Mr. Darcy's Pledge

Volume I
of
THE DARCY NOVELS

Monica Fairview

Other Books by Monica Fairview
The Other Mr. Darcy
The Darcy Cousins
Steampunk Darcy
An Improper Suitor (Regency)

Mr. Darcy's Pledge
Copyright © 2014 by Monica Fairview

An Imprint of White Soup Press

Chapter One

Mrs. Annesley spotted the carriage as it took the turning, before it disappeared behind the trees. The window from the upstairs parlor was very well situated to enable its occupants to see across the estate, though it would be some time before the carriage would approach Pemberley House.

"I believe that might have been your brother's carriage, Georgiana," said Mrs. Annesley. "I thought I caught a glimpse of maroon, but at this distance it is impossible to be certain."

Georgiana jumped up and ran to the window, though of course it was useless because the carriage would be hidden by the woods until it was almost at their doorstep. "Do you think so? But why would my brother arrive without informing anyone ahead of time? You know how he doesn't like to put the staff to any inconvenience by arriving unexpectedly."

"It may well not be your brother, in which case you should come away from the window before someone catches you staring like a hoyden."

Georgiana did not want to be robbed of a chance to satisfy her curiosity, but she was too well bred to argue with Mrs. Annesley, who was such a kind and caring companion, quite unlike that horrid Mrs. Younge who had betrayed her so badly. Though chomping at the bit with impatience, she had to be satisfied with plucking up her ears and listening with all her might for the sound of approaching carriage wheels.

"Do you think my brother will approve of my new musical composition?" she asked, as much to break into the long silence as to relieve her anxiety.

"My dear Georgiana, you alone are able to judge whether your composition is good or not. Gentlemen like your brother are not as well versed in music as you are. If you are happy with it – and you are harder on yourself than anyone else would be – then I am sure it will please your brother."

Georgiana felt a flush of pleasure. Really, Mrs. Annesley was so kind to her, far kinder than she deserved.

She took up her sewing, focusing on producing a neat stitch, in case she needed to show it to her brother for inspection. Of course Darcy rarely criticized her, but she wanted to impress him, to show him that since that debacle with Wickham, she had not wasted her time in idleness. She had worked very hard to prove herself an accomplished and capable young lady. She desperately wanted him to forget about her stupidity and to look at her without remembering what had almost happened. So far she had not succeeded, to judge by the careful manner in which he always greeted her, but she was determined to make him forget, to convince him that, just because she had proved immature once, it did not mean she would always be that way.

It seemed an age before the approaching carriage began to be heard. She was so consumed by curiosity that she gave up any pretense at embroidery, set aside her frame and sat on her hands to prevent herself from jumping up, though why sitting on her hands would make any difference she wasn't quite sure.

"Can you peek out of the window for me, Mrs. Annesley? Please? Surely it wouldn't be considered forward if *you* did it. We so rarely get unexpected visitors, I'm consumed with curiosity."

Mrs. Annesley rose to her feet, a small smile lifting the corner of her lips. "I was wondering how long you would be able to endure it. You did very well. I do believe you're beginning to overcome your impulsive character. Your brother will be pleased."

If it was her brother. She wished Mrs. Annesley would move more quickly to the window, then chided herself for being impatient. Impatience was akin to impulsiveness, and she was determined to purge herself of both qualities.

Please let it be her brother. She had not seen him since he had left Town to visit Lady Catherine over Easter, which was three months ago.

She took a deep breath and waited. How could it take so long to walk across the small saloon to the window? Really, was Mrs. Annesley trying to torment her?

Finally, the footsteps stopped and Mrs. Annesley twitched back the curtain to look out.

"It is your brother," she said, turning to Georgiana, a twinkle in her eye.

Georgiana jumped up and hurried downstairs, too excited to even pretend to be patient.

~~X~~

For a man to conquer himself is the first and noblest of victories.

It was one of the few mottoes from Aristotle (or was it Plato?) that Darcy still remembered from the torment of his Ancient Greek classes, and he had repeated it over and over again in the last few weeks. He would never have thought that learning Greek could possibly have any practical usage, but here he was today, clinging to that phrase like a drowning sailor clings to a rope tossed from his ship.

Conquering himself was his only hope of overcoming the madness that had beset him when he had allowed his passion to dominate his thoughts. Still now, after almost three months of thinking about it, he could hardly believe he had been foolish enough to propose to Miss Elizabeth Bennet. It had been a moment of insanity. Much as he had suffered for it after her refusal, he knew now that she, at least, had taken the wise course by turning him down. Heavens be thanked!

He just wished it didn't hurt so much.

The thundering of the horses' hooves echoed the thundering of Fitzwilliam Darcy's heart, the discomfort of the rattling carriage providing distraction from the turmoil inside him. He had urged the coachman to pick up speed on this last stretch towards Pemberley. The coachman, the young son of Ebenezer Saddler who had recently retired, had brightened up at the challenge and taken him at his word. Darcy found it in himself to pity the horses, who would soon reach an exhaustion matching his own, but he needed to reach his home, to bury himself there, as he had done in the days following his father's death. Pemberley, he was sure, would soothe his pain and bring him peace.

A red grouse rose up in protest as the carriage passed it, flying up towards the window with startled mutterings and breaking into Darcy's thoughts. The thick scent of heather filled the carriage, alerting him to the fact that he was reaching the open moor that preceded Pemberley. There was nothing to see here beyond the pale plump forms of grazing sheep that went on for several miles. He waited impatiently for the moor to give way to pink sainfoin and grass fields ready for the harvest.

His chest tightened at the familiar sight. He was home at last. Only, it was not really home, not when there was no one waiting for him. Georgiana was there now, true, but she spent very little time overall in Derbyshire, and in any case she wasn't expecting him.

Pemberley was a large hollow house full of people who were paid to serve him.

The pace of the carriage slowed. Field hands stopped working when they recognized the Darcy crest on his carriage and lifted their hats or bobbed to him. His father had always taught him to greet the workers properly, so he pulled down the window as far as it would go and moved his hand in greeting as he passed.

The carriage speed picked up again once they had entered Pemberley Woods. The roads were kept in excellent repair here and young Ebenezer gave the team free rein.

They were almost there. They rounded the corner, taking it so dangerously fast that the carriage tilted sideways at an alarming angle. For a moment, Darcy thought they would topple. A fierce gladness gripped him. At least losing consciousness would mean losing the obsessive image of Miss Elizabeth Bennet that haunted his mind.

But the carriage did not topple. It continued on its way, barely checking its speed, and Darcy had to admire the skill of young Ebenezer. He was relieved that they had not been overthrown after all. What was he thinking? Being injured and immobile would only make matters worse, leaving him with nothing else to occupy his mind. And being dead – he hoped he had not sank so low yet to wish for that.

No, he had to reach home and he had to keep himself so constantly occupied that he would not have a minute to think. Or at least, to be able to focus on the one thing that gave him a sense of purpose, the one thing he knew with absolute certainty would banish Elizabeth Bennet from his mind forever.

Ah, there was the 300-year-old oak tree that hid Pemberley from view. As they thundered onwards, past the thick trunk marked with dozens of lovers' initials, Pemberley burst into sight like a sweet haven, its two long round columns holding up the roof like a giant's legs. That was how he used to think of them when he was a child. His tutor had told him the legend of Atlas, carrying the world on his shoulders. Fired up by the tale, Darcy's imagination had transformed the vast columns of Pemberley into Atlas's legs. When he had mentioned this to his tutor, the tutor had dismissed the notion, arguing quite logically that if Atlas was holding up the world, he could not possibly be inside it as well, but Darcy clung stubbornly to the idea, convincing himself that they were visible only to a few privileged mortals who could see them. This had lasted a few weeks until Wickham had mocked him in front of a few of the neighborhood boys. Their laughter had finally forced him to accept that it wasn't likely.

This was another ghost constantly haunting him. He would never be rid of Wickham, it seemed. Everywhere he went, Wickham was there to taunt him. How could Miss Bennet have given any credit to Wickham's words? She was an intelligent young woman. How could someone like her be taken in by Wickham's lies? What was it that Wickham possessed that turned intelligent young ladies like Miss Bennet and Georgiana into fools?

He supposed he couldn't blame them. He'd seen many an intelligent man fall victim to a pretty face, and no matter how much he wished that wasn't the case, Wickham was certainly in possession of a fine figure. Wickham had always been able to charm his way into the servants' hearts – as well as old Mr. Darcy's – and charm his way out of many scrapes that should have earned him a whipping but never did.

Already he felt some of the peace of Pemberley slide into him, cool shade on a hot day, although perhaps it was simply the respite from the sun offered by the branches forming a canopy over the road. Darcy signaled with a thump of his walking stick for the coachman to slow down. It would not do for him to gallop up to the entrance at a breakneck pace. He did not wish to alarm Mrs. Reynolds and especially not old Timmons, the butler. It was bad enough that he had given them no notice of his arrival.

Immediately, almost magically, the pace slackened, and they passed through the gateway at a suitably sedate speed.

Georgiana, too, had been surprised. He had considered sending her an express the day before he left London, but had decided against it. If she knew he was coming, she would be full of anticipation; he did not think he could handle the weight of her expectations at this particular moment in time. As it was, he would take her by surprise, and he would tell her immediately of his plans. He had rehearsed the words carefully, all the way down from Town. He had thought at length about what he would say to prepare his sister, though he wished he didn't have to say anything at all, but disguise of any sort was his abhorrence. Once he said the words, there would be no turning back. His life would undergo a dramatic change.

He was glad Georgiana had finished her schooling and that he was not returning to an empty house, though his sister, being much younger, was not quite the companion he could have wished for. For a brief moment, he pictured Miss Elizabeth Bennet as Mrs. Darcy, her eyes laughing as she ran out into the driveway to welcome him home, slipping her arms around his neck. She would lift her face towards him and he would bend down to cover her lips with his own.

The carriage halted and he was jolted back into reality.

There was no Mrs. Darcy, not in the form of Miss Bennet, in any case. But there would be a Mrs. Darcy soon, in another form and shape.

Meanwhile, he had to focus on the here and now. The servants were running out, taken by surprise at his unexpected arrival, quickly scrambling into parallel lines to welcome him, old Timmons looking severe and proper in his dark tailcoat, Mrs. Reynolds smiling as she had always done when he was a child, her wrinkled cheeks more familiar to him than his mother's.

Well, he could not have Elizabeth, but the comfort of the familiar faces brought a choked sensation to his throat.

Then Georgiana stepped out, looking charmingly young and pretty in a white muslin dress with a green sash, her blond hair made up into the elaborate braids that were all the rage in London. She came quickly to him and he thought – *she has grown again. Will my little sister never stop growing?*

He took her into his arms and swung her around.

"I hope you have been employing your time well, little Sister?"

"Of course, Brother. I have a new painted table to show you. And I have a new composition to play, if you are willing to listen."

"I am all ears," he said, placing her hand on his arm and nodding his greeting to the liveried footmen as he passed them.

Darcy turned to Mrs. Annesley, who stood just inside the doorway regarding them with a slight smile on her face. She curtseyed and he bowed to her, infinitely grateful she had agreed to act as companion to his sister.

"I hope your charge has not been giving you trouble," he said.

"None at all," replied Mrs. Annesley. "She is a charming young lady."

Clearly the two had taken to each other, which was all he could have hoped for. Mrs. Annesley was a widow, a very distant relation – so distant he had had to draw out an elaborate family tree to work out how they were related – but she was proving herself indispensable. In just a short time, he had noticed a positive change in the way Georgiana conducted herself.

"Are you staying long this time, Brother?" said Georgiana.

"I am not sure how long I am to stay this time, but I hope to spend a great deal more time in Pemberley in the future," he replied, trying his best to smile. Oh, why was this so difficult? He had practiced the words for several hours. He needed to say them out loud in order to make them real.

He took a deep breath, and before he could change his mind, he blurted out the words.

"Georgiana, I have come to a decision. It is time for me to find a bride for Pemberley."

Who that bride would be, he had no idea. Only one thing was certain. It would not be Elizabeth Bennet.

Chapter Two

Georgiana was not sure what to make of her brother's declaration. He had said it in such a serious manner he made it sound like a momentous decision, whereas it was a possibility she had thought about quite often. Though it worried her that her brother would be bringing a stranger into the house, she had been expecting it for some time. After all, it was time for him to marry, as their Aunt Catherine constantly reminded him; he needed to produce an heir to Pemberley.

Consequently, she was not quite as impressed by his remark as he might have expected.

"Yes, Brother," she said, wondering about the intense look on his face. "But for now, would you like to come in and partake of some refreshments? I am sure some spruce beer is just the thing for this kind of weather."

He seemed surprised at her response. Perhaps she ought to have paid what he said more attention. It was so difficult to know quite how to respond to these things. Mrs. Annesley assured her that she would learn these things as she grew older, but she sometimes despaired of ever doing so.

"You must tell me more about this new plan of yours to find a bride," said Georgiana, trying to make amends. "Do you have someone in mind?"

A shuttered expression crossed his face.

"No. Nobody."

Again, she had the feeling that she was missing something crucial. She felt at a loss. She was not usually tongue-tied in her brother's presence, but today he seemed different, almost a stranger.

"Shall I ring for spruce beer, then?"

He waved his hand. "First I will go upstairs to change, then I will join you by and by for a cup of tea and a cold repast."

Food was clearly the last thing on her brother's mind however, when he joined her later. For a while, as the servants entered with cold meat, cake and fruits, they were silent. Meanwhile, her brother sat a distracted air and seemed to start whenever she tried to engage him in conversation.

"Are you not hungry, Brother, after your journey?" said Georgiana. She had had refreshments brought up, but beyond a small sip of tea, Darcy had not touched a morsel.

"I dined at the Red Stag," said Darcy. "Cold meats and ale. I have not had the chance to be hungry yet."

Yet he was the one who had mentioned the cold repast.

She had sensed a false heartiness to his manner when he had first arrived. What little there had been of it had already been abandoned. He now sat silently in his habitual armchair, staring into his teacup. Georgiana cast a glance towards Mrs. Annesley, who was quietly occupied with her sewing. She wondered if her companion had noticed anything amiss with Darcy or if it was just her own imagination. Perhaps it was something to do with his decision to find a wife. Perhaps he felt compelled to marry but was not quite ready to do so.

She wanted to ask him more about his sudden determination, but knew better than to intrude. He would explain, she supposed, in his own good time.

At least he had informed her of his intensions. Beyond that, she would simply have to content herself with believing that Darcy knew what he was doing and would never choose someone unsuitable.

To avoid any appearance of prying into his private affairs, Georgiana decided to focus on a safe topic: Darcy's trip to Rosings, which he had hardly mentioned in his letters.

"You did not write to me about your stay at Rosings, William," said Georgiana. "How does our aunt Catherine fare? Is she the same as always? Did she bring up the subject of your dead body?" She gave a little laugh. It was a joke they shared. When Darcy was around fifteen, he had had an outburst in which he had informed Lady Catherine that he would marry Anne over his dead body. Since Darcy had told Georgiana the story, it had become their private joke, and they referred to their aunt's marriage plans as his dead body.

"My dead body?" Darcy looked completely blank.

What was wrong with him? Mrs. Annesley cast a sharp glance at Georgiana and she felt silly. Was she being childish? Was it not appropriate to mention their joke?

"William, you know what I mean!" she said, laughing uneasily. "I'm referring of course to your proposal."

Darcy turned pale, as if she'd exposed a hideous secret to the world.

"My proposal?"

"Oh, I'm sorry," she said, feeling she ought to be contrite but not quite sure why. "Perhaps I ought not to have spoken of it in front of Mrs. Annesley, but surely it is not so very dire."

"Who told you about my proposal?" He was staring at her with an intensity that was most perplexing.

Then she realized what had happened. She was all astonishment, not quite able to get her thoughts round this new development.

"No. Darcy. Tell me you did not!"

He was engaged to their cousin Anne. No wonder he had been behaving so strangely. She had nothing against Anne. Nothing at all. She pitied her, if anything. But to think of her brother as permanently shackled to a lady who barely spoke two words at a time was too much. It was unfair to Pemberley. It was unfair to *her*. Darcy deserved better. She knew Lady Catherine had rather forceful powers of persuasion, but she had thought Darcy immune to them. How had Aunt Catherine managed to browbeat her brother into doing the deed?

She could not blame him for being reluctant to speak of his bride.

Darcy sprang to his feet and came over to her. He held her by the arms and peered at her closely with such an agitated expression that she was more convinced than ever that, somehow, Aunt Catherine had coerced him into an agreement.

"I have spoken out of turn, Brother," she said, gently. "Of course you are entitled to choose your own bride. You hardly need my permission."

"What have you heard?" he said.

"I have heard nothing," she answered, confused. "News reaches us slowly in Derbyshire, as you are only too aware. I have merely deduced from your manner that Lady Catherine has finally convinced you to propose to our cousin."

He let go of her as abruptly as he had seized her. "Our cousin? Lady Catherine? Are you referring to Anne?" He threw back his head and laughed. "You must be mad to think I would do such a thing."

He looked immensely relieved. "Is that all?" said Darcy, smiling as he went to stand by the window. "You are acquainted with me well enough, I hope, to know I would not submit to Lady Catherine in this matter, irrespective of the pressure she brought to bear. Rest assured that I will never bring Cousin Anne to Pemberley as a bride."

He sounded almost cheerful, but now that he stood in full daylight she could see there were shadows under his eyes and he had lost weight since she last saw him.

"Enough talk of disagreeable subjects," said Darcy, with false heartiness. "I believe you promised to play your newest composition to me."

There was nothing more she would have liked to do than to play him her music, but her mind was in whirl. What had happened to make him react so oddly to her question? She cast her mind back to what she had said, but could not make head or tail of Darcy's behavior. She did not think she could play very calmly when her brother was so agitated.

"Your composition is very soothing. I am sure your brother will find it to his taste," prompted Mrs. Annesley. "You need not be shy about playing it, Georgiana. Would you like me to turn the pages for you?"

Mrs. Annesley put down her embroidery, walked to the piano, and began to arrange the music. Accustomed as she was to obedience, Georgiana followed, trying her best to clear her mind. She struggled to focus on the neat notations she had written.

With no other choice left to her, she began to play, and as usual, she found the notes an oasis of calm. She had discovered music after the incident with Wickham. She had drawn solace from her disappointment and embarrassment by losing herself in the piano keys as the gentle sound rose up from them to envelope her and shield her from the world.

As the last note evaporated into the air and the music ended, she waited for the expected applause. There was a long silence that stretched out for so long she almost despaired of a reaction.

Darcy was still at the window, but his back was turned to her and he was just a dark silhouette against the daylight.

"William?" she said.

At the sound of his name, Darcy turned to her and began to applaud.

"Well done, little sister. That was beautiful. You have become a truly accomplished musician."

He did not fool her one little bit. He had not heard a note of her playing.

As long as she had known him, she had never had occasion to believe he was not listening to her music. It was one of the constants of her life to have her brother's admiration for her music.

There was something wrong with her brother, and she intended to find out what it was.

~~X~~

Pleading a headache, Darcy withdrew to the library, hoping to distract himself by looking over some estate matters. But he was too restless, and the dark mahogany library with its smell of books and dust, its tall shelves packed to the brim – the sense of airlessness to the room – everything contributed to making him feel hemmed in. He felt guilty, too, for abandoning his sister so soon after arriving when he knew how much she looked forward to his company.

It was not long before the guilt got the better of him and he went in search of Georgiana. She was playing the piano softly. Mrs. Annesley was snoozing in an armchair, her white matron's cap all askew, her sewing hanging halfway off her lap.

The moment Georgiana saw him she put a finger to her lips and, with a smiling look towards her companion, she took his hand and they tiptoed together out of the room like naughty children.

"I'm so glad you came back, for I was feeling a little out of sorts. Mrs. Annesley is a wonderful companion, but in the afternoons she tends to grow drowsy and then I am left to my own devices. May I show you the table I painted? I only finished it two days ago. I worked especially hard on it, hoping to finish it before you joined us at Pemberley."

"I'd love to see it," said Darcy.

The table really was a very fine piece. The delicate details were exquisitely rendered and far exceeded the usual accomplishments young ladies produced.

"It is amazing to me," said Bingley, "how young ladies can have the patience to be so very accomplished as they all are."

"All young ladies accomplished! My dear Charles, what do you mean?"

"Yes, all of them, I think. They all paint tables, cover screens, and net purses. I scarcely know anyone who cannot do all this, and I am sure I never heard a young lady spoken of for the first time, without being informed that she was very accomplished." ...

"All this she must possess," added Darcy, "and to all this she must yet add something more substantial, in the improvement of her mind by extensive reading."

"I am no longer surprised at your knowing only six accomplished women. I rather wonder now at your knowing any."

"Are you so severe upon your own sex as to doubt the possibility of all this?"

"I never saw such a woman. I never saw such capacity, and taste, and application, and elegance, as you describe united."

So that was what Elizabeth Bennet believed? Well he would prove her wrong. He would find an accomplished woman with all those abilities and more, and he would prove her wrong. There were far more accomplished ladies in the world than Elizabeth Bennet could imagine in her limited social sphere. She did not have the advantage of moving in the first circles.

"I can see from your expression that you don't like it," said Georgiana. "You're scowling. Don't worry. You are not obliged to say anything nice. I will consign the table to the attic."

"You will do no such thing, Georgiana. I am nursing a raging headache. I believe the heat is having a bad effect on me. That is why I am scowling – if that is indeed what I am doing. It has nothing to do with your artwork. It so happens I think you are an enormously talented young woman. I will ask the servants to carry the table upstairs – not to the attic, but to display it in the Picture Gallery amongst the professional paintings."

Georgiana blushed with pleasure.

"You are teasing me, brother."

"I am not teasing you. You know me to be completely truthful, do you not?"

She nodded slowly, in that uncertain way of hers that indicated that she did not quite believe him.

"When I think of all the accomplished ladies you meet in town," she said, "I feel I cannot possibly compete with them. They are all so graceful and well-dressed, and so sure of themselves. How can I possibly move among them and be noticed? I am sure that if I am invited to a dance, I shall be slighted by all the gentlemen in favor of more elegant females than I."

I am in no humor at present to give consequence to young ladies who are slighted by other men.

Had he really pronounced such words within Miss Bennet's hearing? Had he really been so arrogant and unfeeling? Much as he wished those words unsaid, he knew that he was guilty of saying them. No wonder she had made so little effort to answer his proposal with any delicacy – she had considered him too callous to be hurt by her words. If someone had said those words to Georgiana, what impact might they have had?

Georgiana would have been devastated.

Yet he had spoken them quite openly, within a young lady's hearing.

No wonder that young lady had turned him down.

Now here was his sister, seeking reassurances. He wanted her to realize how handsome and remarkable she was but he did not know how. How could a few words of his convince Georgiana of her value? He was fumbling in the dark. For the first time in many years he had doubts about his ability to play the role of guardian. How could he, when he had never given a thought to the effect his words might have on others?

His proposal, for an example. He flinched as he thought of the tactless words he had uttered. He remembered well how he had waxed eloquent on his sense of Elizabeth Bennet's inferiority— of its being a *degradation* to even consider marriage to her.

He could not blame her for thinking him the most insensitive man in her experience.

Yet here was Georgiana, who hung upon his every word and for whom an unkind word was like a final sentence. He had never before thought of it this way. He had to be a father to Georgiana as well as a mother, and he was not particularly suited to either role, because he did not have a way with words the way people like Wickham did. That was why it had been so easy for Wickham to steal his little sister's affection. Wickham could weave words like a spell to capture his victims.

How could words have so much importance? It was why a gentleman's word was his honor. So much depended on it.

"Georgiana," he said. "When you have your Season, you will outshine all the young ladies in London. I can guarantee you that you will more than likely have the opposite problem. I will be plagued with suitors and I will be forced to waste a great deal of my time and energy in turning them away."

It was entirely true. Unfortunately, it would not be just her good looks, or her accomplishments, or her sweet nature that would attract the gentlemen. It would be her fortune as well, and the trick was to discover who was sincere in his courtship and who was not.

"Do you really think so, William? But how am I to know whether they truly like me or whether in fact they like my fortune?"

At least her disaster with Wickham had been useful in one thing. She would not be so easily deceived again.

"You must rely on your judgment and perception, little Sister. You are too wise now to be fooled by pretty words."

She pressed her lips together and for a moment she looked so vulnerable Darcy wanted to wrap his arms around her and take the pain away, but she was too old now to be comforted by something so simple. Besides, she needed to finally put the past behind her and look to the future.

She was no longer that fifteen-year-old who had almost succumbed to Wickham's charms. She would be turning seventeen soon, and it would be time for her to look for a husband.

With a shock he realized her Season was not that long away. His little sister was no longer little. At seventeen, she could make her come-out.

When had the time flown? It seemed like only yesterday that she had been a child who had lost both parents and was looking to him to take care of her. He had always promised himself to spend more time with her. But in between her schooling and his life as a young gentleman, they had spent too little time together.

Now it was almost too late.

Then another realization struck him. How in Heaven's name was Georgiana to have her Season? Georgiana needed a chaperone – a lady, obviously -- who would help prepare her wardrobe and accompany her to dances and balls and all the places young ladies went to when they were debutantes. He could not chaperone her himself.

Which led him again to the same conclusion. The old adage *Omnes viae Romam ducunt – all roads lead to Rome –* seemed to apply very well here. In this case, it was all roads lead to marriage.

He needed to find a wife, not only for his own sake, but for Georgiana's sake, and the task of doing so was more urgent than ever.

Chapter Three

It was a warm, sticky night, one of those summer nights when, even with the windows open, it was difficult to breathe. When Darcy finally managed to drift off, after what seemed like hours of waiting in vain for sleep to overcome him, a clap of thunder roused him. He trudged to the windows to close them. The rain provided no relief from the heat; quite the opposite. With the windows closed, the room grew even more oppressive.

His brief periods of slumber were flooded with torrid dreams that ended in disappointment. In one particularly vivid dream, he thought Elizabeth was running towards him, but as he reached out to embrace her, he realized she was looking behind him at Wickham. In the dream, he was compelled to look on as Wickham came forward to seize her and plant his lips on hers.

Darcy sat up in his bed and ran his hands over his face in despair. Now both Wickham and Elizabeth were invading his dreams. Even if he was able to control his thoughts in the daytime, he could not control them at night.

It simply would not do. Something had to be done about it before long or he feared for his sanity.

The only way he would be able to forget Elizabeth was to replace her with a real-life bride. The problem was he did not wish to be hasty in his choice. He could not allow himself to be ruled either by passion or desperation. He wanted to choose calmly and rationally.

What then was he waiting for?

The sooner he decided what an ideal bride for Pemberley should be like, the sooner he could begin his search.

Full of determination, he rose and dressed without the assistance of his valet. Sequestering himself in the library, he sat at his desk, sharpened a quill, and began to write.

List of Requirements for a Wife

This would be easy enough. He had no doubt that, in the course of the next half hour, his list would be ready. How difficult could it be, after all, to define the qualities one wished for in a wife?

"You must comprehend a great deal in your idea of an accomplished woman."

"Yes, I do comprehend a great deal in it."

"Oh! certainly," cried Caroline, "no one can be really esteemed accomplished who does not greatly surpass what is usually met with. A woman must have a thorough knowledge of music, singing, drawing, dancing, and the modern languages, to deserve the word; and besides all this, she must possess a certain something in her air and manner of walking, the tone of her voice, her address and expressions, or the word will be but half deserved."

"All this she must possess," added Darcy, "and to all this she must yet add something more substantial, in the improvement of her mind by extensive reading."

"I am no longer surprised at your knowing only six accomplished women. I rather wonder now at your knowing any."

Her face, full of scorn, rose up before him. So she would mock his list? He gritted his teeth, gripped the quill tightly, and wrote the first item.

One: Tolerably handsome.

She did not have to be beautiful, but if she was to distract him from Elizabeth Bennet—.

Not handsome enough to tempt me.

How wrong he had been! She had made him eat his words. Now he considered her the standard of beauty by which he would measure every woman.

He pictured her before him – her laughing eyes, her smile, the playful toss of the brown ringlets surrounding her face, her rounded figure, slim in just the right places—

He struck his hand against the desk. There he was again, thinking of *her* instead of imagining the lady who would soon be taking her place next to him.

The blow dislodged the quill and splattered ink all over his list, a big blotch covering the word *handsome*. He crumpled up the paper and threw it away, then began painstakingly again.

List of Requirements for a Wife.

He stared at it for a while, but nothing came to mind.

He pushed back his chair and rose. What he needed was activity. He had spent too much time confined to a carriage over the last two days. A fast gallop across the fields was all he needed to clear his mind.

~~x~~

The weather was perfect for a ride. He had not ridden Derby Spirit for a while. The bay was clearly happy to see him and eager to exercise. It was just cool enough to be a pleasant contrast to the heat the night before. Grey clouds covered the sun, though a patchwork of blue sky towards the south promised more sunshine later. Precipitation from the thunderstorm last night lingered in the air, rising in a soft mist from the ground as the day grew warmer. Rainwater nestled in the leaves, cascading over Darcy every time he brushed against a branch. The meadows around him glistened with miniature pearls of moisture.

As he traversed the valley along the meandering banks of the river Derwent, the crooning of the water was balm to his soul. He had forgotten how beautiful his land was – framed as it was by a sharp ascent on one side, the soft green plain of the valley on the other, and then, rising gently again, the verdant hills speckled with grazing sheep. How could he be unhappy, when all was as it should be, as it had always been?

He transitioned her up to a canter then allowed her free rein as she moved into a gallop. The sense of freedom as the cooling air brushed

22

past them, the open spaces, the familiar sights along the way – all brought him back to the here and now and, for a moment, the tightness inside him eased.

There was peace here, peace and tranquility, if he could only hold onto it. He was the proud owner of a magnificent estate, passed down from generation to generation. What did the contempt of one woman signify in the midst of all this grandeur?

He took a fence slightly too low – nothing serious, but enough to cause Spirit's hoof to skim the fence. He held her back then, slowed her into a running walk. He did not want to injure his horse because of his own upheaval.

He rode past his own estate in the direction of the village. There were people in Lambton he needed to speak to. It was always good to keep good relations between the estate and the businesses in the village and to drop into the local inn to discover the latest news.

The public bridleway passed within view of Houghton Park, the Renwicks' estate. Sir Charles Renwick was a baronet. Darcy's mother had been a particular friend of Mrs. Renwick – they had come out the same year, and their initial friendship was sealed by the fact that they had given birth to sons within months of each other. Edward Renwick had been his playmate for many years.

Darcy felt a stab of grief as he remembered his old friend. Edward had died in the Peninsula fighting Napoleon, having defied his parents' wishes by joining the army in spite of being an only son. The funeral had been the last time he had seen the Renwicks; they had withdrawn from society afterwards, not even attending church on Sundays.

That had been three years ago.

It occurred to him now that Lady Renwick would be the perfect person to sponsor Georgiana's come-out. That was, if he could convince her to do so. It was not a far-fetched preposition. Lady Renwick had been a close friend of his mother's. He recalled overhearing a conversation between her and his father.

"When the day comes, Mr. Darcy, I will be more than happy to take Georgiana to London for her Season. I'm sure Lady Anne would have wished me to do so, particularly as I have no daughters of my own to launch."

"I cannot think of a better person to support my daughter as she transforms from a child into a woman, except for her mother, of course," his father had said.

Perhaps Darcy could remind her of that exchange, if she seemed reluctant. Obviously, as she was in mourning, she would not initially like the idea. But it was just possible that fulfilling her promise to assist her old friend's daughter might give her just the reason she needed to set aside her mourning and re-enter society. She had no daughters of her own It would fulfil a double purpose. Lady Renwick would play a mother's role by presenting her at Court and chaperoning her at parties, while at the same time Darcy would be helping her recover from her morning and giving her a reason to return to normal life.

He urged his horse onwards and turned onto the familiar pathway through the woods leading to Houghton House.

Who knows? She may know of a suitable bride for me. I cannot endure many more nights of torment like last night.

~~X~~

The butler who appeared in the doorway gave no sign of recognizing Darcy. Instead he took Darcy's calling card, bowed stiffly, and told him to wait.

Darcy half expected to be turned away. He spent the time going over arguments in his head, trying to think of what he could say to Lady Renwick, to convince her to help him out.

If she turned him away, he would write her a letter, explaining the reason for his intrusion, and begging her to help him out with his sister.

To his relief, however, when the butler reappeared, he asked him to follow.

This is good sign. Something good will come of it.

Sir Charles and Lady Renwick received him in the parlor. All the windows were closed and the air had a dusty, oppressive feel to it. Lady

Renwick was dressed in lavender, choosing to remain in half-mourning despite the passage of three years. Sir Charles was sitting in an armchair reading a book on angling. He had aged a great deal.

"I am sorry to call on you so unexpectedly," said Darcy. "I hope you will forgive the intrusion."

"You are the son of my dearest friend Anne, and a friend of my son, Mr. Darcy. I hope you will always feel welcome here."

Sir Thomas muttered a few words of greeting and turned his gaze to his book.

"Sir Thomas does not go out much in society," said Lady Renwick, in a half-whisper. "You must excuse him if he is unfriendly. He tends to prefer reading over conversation."

"We all become attached to certain habits," remarked Darcy.

"Oh, you are far too young to have acquired any habits," said Lady Renwick, with a smile. "But it is kind of you to say so."

There was a pause, in which Darcy felt awkward. Now that he was here, he was uncertain how to proceed.

"I suspect you are here to ask me something?" said Lady Renwick. "Does it have anything to do with your mother?"

"Yes. No. Not directly. I have come to ask you if you will assist me with Georgiana. In the first place, I am at a loss as how to introduce her to the neighborhood. I am well acquainted with the gentlemen of the area, of course, but I do not know the ladies, and know of no way of bridging the gap. I know you are in mourning, but I am hoping that you would be willing to help her at least set up a guest list for an entertainment we are planning."

He would not mention the Season just yet. One step at a time. He wasn't even sure Lady Renwick would want to do anything at all.

"You have called at a fortunate moment," said Lady Renwick. "I have in fact recently decided to cast off my mourning – not of course because I mourn Edward any less, but because I have been given a new responsibility. I have promised my sister – who is recovering from a severe illness — to sponsor my niece in her forthcoming Season in London and to present her at Court. She is coming to stay with me for a few weeks so we can grow to know each other. I was already forming plans to introduce her in the neighborhood. So your request comes at a remarkably good time, especially since my niece arrived only yesterday."

"Then I am fortunate indeed," said Darcy, politely, but he was disappointed. If she was bringing out her niece, it would be too much to expect her to sponsor his sister as well. But at least she could help Georgiana forge connections with some of the families around them.

"I would be happy to call on you and your sister with my niece to discuss the possibilities further, if that would be agreeable to you."

"Of course."

"In a day or two, then."

Darcy rose. "I will await your visit." He bowed.

"What, leaving already?" said Sir Thomas, looking up from his book.

"It was merely a quick call," said Darcy. "Would you care to join me in some fishing, Sir Thomas? I would welcome the company and the river is well stocked."

"I might take you up on that, my boy," said Sir Thomas, with sudden unexpected liveliness. "I've been reading about a new type of fly. I'd like to try my luck with it."

Just then there was a quick step outside the door.

"Ah, that must be my niece. You will have the privilege of being the first in the neighborhood to meet her."

Suddenly, right before him, was the most beautiful creature Darcy had ever set eyes on. With a tall symmetrical figure, a swan's grace, and aristocratic features – arched brows and an aquiline nose – she gave off a general air of confidence. Her clothes were the height of fashion.

"Allow me to introduce Miss Elinor Marshall. Elinor, this is Mr. Fitzwilliam Darcy, of Pemberley."

"Delighted to meet you, Mr. Darcy."

Her courtesy was all elegance.

Perhaps finding a bride might not be as difficult as he had thought after all.

Chapter Four

Darcy awoke the next morning refreshed and with a sense that the worst was behind him. For the first time for many months he did not awake with Elizabeth's face in his imagination. He was so relieved that he had finally forgotten about her that he began to whistle.

As if in response, a thrush outside began to warble. Darcy lingered in bed for a while, listening to its clear, piping song, noticing how it repeated the same phrases over.

It had been a long time since he had listened to a bird singing.

It had been a long time since he had noticed *life*.

Surely this was a sign that his brooding period was over, and he was about to embark on a fresh start?

Even his valet noticed there was a change.

"Well, Mr. Darcy," said his valet, as he straightened Darcy's sleeves. "It's a pleasure to see you shake off the doldrums, sir. Is there a particular reason for it?"

"I hope so, Briggs, I hope so. I have decided to hold a house party. That should liven up this place."

"A house party? Other than the one you normally have this time of the year?"

"Yes, a real house party."

"That is excellent news, sir. It's been a long time since we had a proper house party at Pemberley. Are you inviting a great many guests?"

No doubt Briggs wanted to know as much as possible so he could break the news below stairs, but Darcy did not have an answer. He had only just thought of the idea, but now it had taken hold and he was firmly convinced it was an answer to many of his problems.

It would be excellent practice for Georgiana, who would be compelled to play hostess, and an opportunity to meet some young gentlemen from the district. Nothing too big, nothing too elaborate. He would put Georgiana in charge of the arrangements, a task which would help her develop her skills in managing a household. And at the end of the house party, he would hold a formal dance, as Bingley had done at Netherfield, inviting all the eligible young ladies and gentlemen of the neighborhood.

It would give Darcy an opportunity to look around to see if there was anyone who would meet his requirements locally – like Miss Marshall, for example. It would be ideal if he could meet someone before the beginning of the Season. That way he would have someone to help him bring out Georgiana.

No sooner had he thought of the idea, than a host of problems presented themselves. He himself had never held a dance at Pemberley. He had hosted a number of small hunting parties, but they had been bachelor affairs held when Georgiana was away at the Young Ladies Academy. His father had rarely held parties himself, and Darcy remembered very little about the occasions when his mother had entertained guests. He had not been of an age to be interested.

Consequently, Darcy had scarcely more experience in this area than Georgiana. Mrs. Annesley would no doubt be able to help with the actual arrangements, but the real question was to know who to invite. Darcy knew most of the families in the area, particularly those gentlemen with whom he had had dealings of a practical nature, but his status as a bachelor had made it difficult to be on visiting terms with the matrons and young ladies.

Unfortunately, he could think of only one person that could help him on both accounts. Lady Matlock. He did not like having to turn to her for help and he particularly did not wish to have to deal with his uncle the Earl of Matlock, but really, it was his only possibility. The trick was to try and get as much information from them as possible without giving these particular Fitzwilliam relatives a chance to actually interfere.

He would take Georgiana with him. His uncle and aunt would be pleased with the improvements she had made over the last year, and her presence would prevent them from asking too many personal questions.

Lady Matlock had a tendency to think herself entitled to know every detail of his life in London.

They would be pleased that he was making an effort to procure a mistress for Pemberley.

He strode down the corridor to Georgiana's bedchamber. She would be having chocolate in bed, as she was accustomed to doing. He wanted to set out for Cragsmead immediately.

Action. That was what he needed. He had been stagnant for far too long.

~~X~~

Georgiana listened to Darcy's long explanation with alarm. This latest plan was only one more form of proof that something serious was wrong with Darcy. Either that, or it was not Darcy who stood before her but some stranger who resembled him.

Not only had he suddenly decided that she was to host a House Party – a House Party, when she had never even hosted a dinner party! But he had decided that he desperately needed to visit the Fitzwilliams to ask for their assistance.

It was not like normal Darcy to go haring off somewhere at the drop of a hat, and certainly not so soon after arriving from Town, not unless there was an emergency. Consulting with Lady Matlock over a house party did not constitute an emergency, not by any stretch of the imagination.

To make matters even more worrying, normal Darcy always ran *away* from Lady Matlock. Just a whiff of her was enough to send him scurrying in the opposite direction. Her brother in his right mind would never actually *seek out* their uncle and his wife.

She was wise enough not to point out that aspect of things, however.

"But Darcy, you have only just arrived, and you yourself have said that you are plagued by the headache. Surely the last thing you need is another journey."

"A trip to Cragsmead hardly qualifies as a journey, Georgiana. It is less than a half day's ride, and with the warm, dry weather, the roads will be in good condition. Besides, I feel it my duty to call on my uncle. I have not seen him for many months."

"But I have had no time to pack. We need to stay the night at the very least. And besides, don't you thing we should let them know that we are coming? Perhaps it is inconvenient for them to receive us."

"I see no reason to delay. Packing for one or two nights' stay is surely the work of an hour. As for sending ahead, the worse that can happen is that we will be forced to stay the night at an inn. Where is your spirit of adventure, little Sister?"

Adventure and Darcy were not usually terms Georgiana associated with each other. Under regular circumstances, Darcy was extremely reluctant to embark on any journey without full preparation. Adventure to Darcy was synonymous with inconvenience. Even when she had been much younger, any suggestion of adventure on her part would usually be met with opposition. If there was one motto Darcy followed religiously, it was the axiom: 'Be prepared.'

Yet here he was, suggesting setting out on a journey with no preparation at all. It boggled the mind.

Georgiana and Mrs. Annesley exchanged quick glances. Georgiana had already confided in her companion her concerns about her brother. Mrs. Annesley had agreed that Darcy was not himself, though she had pursed her lips in a way that showed she knew more about the situation than she was willing to reveal. Georgiana found that particularly annoying. Why did everyone persist in treating her like a child?

She did not press Mrs. Annesley to say anything, however. She would find out by herself. It was part of growing up, and she needed to learn how to draw out her brother and persuade him to talk.

The trip to Cragsmead would be a perfect occasion to discover what her brother was concealing, even if discovering the truth did not make up for the fact that she did not like visiting her uncle and aunt. She had not seen them for some time, but she had a nightmarish memory of one Yuletide when everyone had gathered at Cragsmead, including Lady

Catherine, and she had been severely chastised for accidentally dropping a piece of pudding on the ground and sent to bed early. She had been fourteen at the time and it *still* rankled.

Perhaps she had been oversensitive. It was quite possible that now she was older, she would come to like them better. Certainly as a child she had been terrified of Lady Catherine, but the last time she had visited her, she had not minded so very much. The same could be true with the Fitzwilliams.

By the time Darcy and Georgiana had set out, Georgiana had talked herself into an optimistic frame of mind.

It was a perfect day in any case for a short journey. The weather outside was hot, but a gentle breeze swept through the open windows and kept the carriage cool inside. The sky was cornflower blue and dotted with little sheep-wool clouds. The fields were green with tall undulating waves of grass ready to be made into hay, and the hills were spread with purple heather and yellow gorse. A Merlin hovered for a while to the right of their carriage, high up above, its tail spread out like a fan, then dove down in a mad, headlong flight to capture some ill-fated prey.

She was not going to fret about Darcy for the moment, she decided. He was her older brother, and he was used to taking care of himself. Perhaps she was the one who was behaving oddly. She had to admit she was anxious about the very thought of looking for a husband; she was not at all ready to do it just yet. And she was just as anxious about her brother looking for a wife.

Darcy might have the right idea, after all. It would be useful to talk to someone who could see the whole picture from the outside.

If only it didn't have to be the Fitzwilliams!

Lord Matlock had never adopted the modern style of dress. For as long as Darcy could remember, his uncle had donned a silk frock coat, matching knee breeches and buckled shoes, with his hair powdered and tied back with a ribbon. Lady Matlock, on the other hand, could be

31

counted upon to be bang up to the mark. She spared no expense on her London *modiste,* who ensured that her illustrious client was a walking fashion statement and served as an advertisement for her establishment.

Darcy was struck anew by the incompatibility of the odd couple.

"Do sit down, Darcy," she said, indicating a rather hideous gilded white sofa which proved to be as uncomfortable as it looked. "You, too, Georgiana."

Georgiana sat down next to him, a polite smile pasted on her face.

"Well, this is unexpected," said Lord Matlock. "To what do we owe this unprecedented visit?"

Unprecedented? Darcy searched in his mind for the last time he had spontaneously called upon his uncle. Try as he would, however, he could not dredge up an occasion. The last time he remembered he had been with his father.

"Hardly unprecedented, sir. I have called upon you on numerous occasions." At his uncle's invitation, but that was a mere technicality.

"I will not press the point. We are, of course, delighted to see you. And Georgiana, too. I see my niece has grown. She has reached marriageable age."

"She has, indeed," said Lady Matlock. "And a pretty piece she is, too."

Darcy did not like the speculative look his uncle was giving her. Confound it. Why had he thought it a good idea to involve his uncle in his plans? What if Lord Matlock took it into his mind to marry her to one of his old cronies?

The very idea turned his stomach.

"She is still in the schoolroom, however," said Darcy, ignoring Georgiana's look of protest.

"Yes, yes," said his uncle. "How old is she? Sixteen? I always say, the younger they get married, the better for everyone. Avoids the possibility of scandal and all that."

He felt Georgiana stiffen beside him. Of course his uncle knew nothing about the Wickham business, but his sister had no way of knowing that. He gave her hand a quick reassuring pat.

"My own daughters were married off at sixteen," continued Lord Matlock. "Never even had a Season. We chose their husbands ourselves, and a very good thing, too. They are all suitably married and happily so, having none of the tiresome and impractical expectations out of marriage some young ladies tend to have today."

"Quite," said Lady Matlock. "We don't hold with these newfangled notions of love and romance. It's all very well for the lower orders, but those of our class cannot afford to think of marriage in that way. I hope *you* do not hold such phantasmagoric ideas, Georgiana."

Georgiana shifted in her seat, blushed prettily, and said nothing, which was all that was expected of her.

"The fate of England lies in old families such as ours," said Lord Matlock. "Marriage is an alliance formed for the mutual benefit of two landowners wishing to enhance their holdings. I hope you understand that, Georgiana."

Georgiana gave a little nod.

"Good! Good!" said Lord Matlock. "I can see we shall have no difficulties finding you a husband."

Darcy frowned. He had known his uncle to be a stickler, but could he really be that medieval? A fine pickle he'd landed Georgiana in if Lord and Lady Matlock were to take it upon themselves to marry her off.

"Fortunately," said Darcy, hoping to end the discussion, "Georgiana is independently wealthy and does not need to marry to consolidate her earnings."

"On the contrary, my dear Darcy, her wealth will be the trap to draw the fox and then – snap! She will have made her bed and may prepare to be bedded," said his uncle, with a loud guffaw.

Lady Matlock tittered. "Hush, Lord Matlock, you are making the poor child blush."

"Nonsense, my dear. I dare say she thinks about it all the time," he said, winking at his niece. He wandered over to a side table and waving a snifter at him. "Care for some excellent brandy, Darcy?"

"Yes, sir," he said, though normally he would have objected. He generally preferred not to drink smuggled French brandy. He did not wish to antagonize his uncle, however. Not when Georgiana's future might be at stake.

"As I was saying – the fact that she is independently wealthy only makes it more likely that she would marry well. Why, she could easily find herself a bankrupt peer in need of a boost to the jugular – money, my dear," he said to Georgiana, in response to her small gasp. "I am not speaking literally."

"Quite," said Lady Matlock. "Even a duke could be possible. Though, I am not currently acquainted with a Duke who is bankrupt. Perhaps it need not be a duke."

"It need not be a Duke," said Lord Matlock. "And he need not be bankrupt. The chit's got good looks. With the right clothes—. You know, I think you have hit upon something, my dear. Just leave it to us, Darcy, and we'll take care of the matter for you. We'll have to do something about her manners, however. It would never do to have a Fitzwilliam who is a shrinking violet."

Georgiana was in fact shrinking against Darcy, who was feeling hot under the collar. What insanity had possessed him to bring poor Georgiana into the lion's lair? He had to put an end to this right now, before it went any farther.

"I am exceedingly grateful to you, Uncle, for your consideration, but I prefer not to marry my sister off too early. I would like her to have a Season in London. She has had too little joy in her life with both my father and mother gone, and I do not wish her to enter the marriage state before she had had a chance to see something of the world. Why, if it were not for the war in France, I would even plan to take her on a Grand Tour with me."

Darcy had deliberately brought up the war with France in the hopes that it would distract his uncle, who had a particular dislike of the war because it interfered with several of his pleasures, and the impossibility of a Grand Tour being a particular grievance of his.

"Ah, *now* you are talking like a sensible man, Darcy. The Grand Tour. Napoleon ought be shot for making it so difficult to go on the Grand Tour. I do not believe a gentleman's education can be complete

34

without touring the Continent and availing himself of all that Western Civilization has to offer, particularly the antiquities, in the company of a knowledgeable bear-leader. Paris, Geneva, Turin, Florence, Venice, Naples, Pompeii, Vienna, Heidelberg. Do you remember, my dear, when you and I went on a Grand Tour of our own? Not, of course, the real thing, but we had a whirl of a time, did we not, Lady Matlock."

"Quite," said Lady Matlock. "Naturally not the real thing. There are places a Lady should never visit. I hope you are not planning to take your sister to the Alps, Darcy. Wild, horrid things, all rocks and ravines and goat droppings." She shuddered. "Not at all suitable for a refined young lady."

Darcy refrained from answering that he had no intention of taking Georgiana anywhere as long as there was a war going on. He was only too glad that his uncle had, for the moment at least, forgotten about marrying off Georgiana.

"Do you think we have a chance of defeating Napoleon any time soon, Uncle?"

"That Corsican upstart may be as slippery as an eel, but nothing we can't manage. We gave him a thorough trouncing at sea. We'll give him a thorough trouncing on land. If only the weather weren't so confoundedly hot." He took out a lace-bordered handkerchief and wiped his brow. "It's hard work, fighting in the heat, and it doesn't help when our Spanish allies take it upon themselves to sleep half the day."

"The Spanish have never lifted a finger for England," said Lady Matlock, "other than to produce sherry. You can forgive them almost anything for that. Do you care for sherry, Georgiana?"

"I have not had the opportunity to taste it, Lady Matlock," said Georgiana, flustered at becoming the object of conversation again.

"What, not tasted sherry?" said Lord Matlock. "What were you thinking of, Darcy?"

"To be honest, I was not thinking at all, Uncle."

Lord Matlock gave him a hard stare, as if to determine whether he was joking or not. What Darcy had meant to say, in fact, was that, since he considered Georgiana still a schoolroom miss, he did not think sherry appropriate for her. However, to say so would bring them back to the precisely the same subject he had done his best to avoid. Consequently, he had no further explanation to give to his uncle.

His only concern currently was to remove himself from the premises as soon as possible. He came to his feet, pretending not to notice his aunt's look of surprise, and gave Georgiana's hand a tug. She rose uncertainly.

"I offer my humble apologies, but I am afraid we must depart."

"Nonsense!" said Lord Matlock. "You have only just arrived. Surely you do not intend to return to Pemberley today?"

"Indeed," said Lady Matlock. "I never heard of such a thing. Besides, I have already rung for refreshments."

She folded her hands on her lap with a smug expression, as though that decided matters.

"It so happens," said Darcy, annoyed at having his arm twisted, "that we were on our way to visit a friend of mine in Derby and hope to arrive there by nightfall."

He had told so many lies since he arrived at Cragsmead he was surprised the ground did not open up in front of him and swallow him up. If he stayed a moment longer here he would be in danger of giving up his soul to perdition entirely.

Lady Matlock turned her head away to indicate her displeasure. "Well then. There is nothing further to be said."

Lord Matlock pursed his lips and swirled his brandy around and around in his snifter as he stared hard at his nephew. "Don't think I can't tell when you're shamming it, but for the life of me I can't work out why. Be gone with you, then. Young people these days..."

"Precisely," said Lady Matlock, with a sniff. "And to think, Georgiana does not even have a maid with her. Not quite the thing, you know."

"It is only a very short visit, Aunt," said Darcy. "A maid is not essential."

He bowed politely and, offering Georgiana his arm, walked stiffly out of the room, feeling two pairs of eyes observing him. The moment the footman closed the door behind him, he let out a sigh.

"I am sorry I subjected you to that, Georgiana," he said. "It was an incredibly foolish notion of mine to come here."

What was happening to him? It was as if the moment he had given in to the impulse to propose to Elizabeth Bennet, he had taken leave of his senses – as if the floodgates had opened and now refused to close again. He had driven over to Cragsmead on an impulse, and he had left on an impulse.

He would never have been guilty of such impulsive actions in the past. Rash behavior had always been a characteristic of Charles Bingley that was incomprehensible to him. He remembered when Elizabeth Bennet had tried to turn his criticism of Bingley into a compliment.

"Would Mr. Darcy then consider the rashness of your original intention as atoned for by your obstinacy in adhering to it?"

"Upon my word I cannot exactly explain the matter -- Darcy must speak for himself."

He frowned as he caught himself once again thinking of Miss Bennet.

"You need not scowl, William, it was not as bad as I expected after all," said Georgiana, breaking into his thoughts. "Besides, I am assured of marriage to a bankrupt duke, no less. What more could any young lady wish for?"

Darcy turned to her in astonishment, but by then they had reached their carriage. Leaning against the squabs, he chose his words carefully.

"What more?" he said, hoarsely. "Georgiana, surely you realize you can do better than that. There are other considerations—"

A noise that sounded suspiciously like a snort reached him. He looked over to his sister to find her eyes dancing, her mouth covered by her gloved hand as she tried to contain her laughter.

"Fitzwilliam Darcy! Surely you cannot be so beef witted as to think I meant it!"

He did not know what surprised him most – her use of slang, or her laughter. For a moment he was torn between the need to reprimand her, as he felt he ought, and the impulse to cast caution to the wind and laugh alongside her.

Laughter won. As the team drawing the carriage began to move, he gave in to the impulse and for the next few minutes, Fitzwilliam Darcy forgot about Elizabeth Bennet, forgot he was supposed to be dignified, and allowed himself to dissolve into a fit of laughter.

Chapter Five

Darcy was going through his correspondence when a note arrived from Lady Renwick, informing him that she intended to call that day with her niece.

He waited for a spark to happen, a reaction, a small thrill of anticipation to indicate that Miss Marshall had made an impact on him, but he felt nothing.

He sighed. He would be a fool to expect too much of himself.

The main thing is that he was taking the first tentative steps towards matrimony. He was solving his problems. He was taking action. All these were good. He had only been in Pemberley a few days and he had accomplished a great deal. His visit to Cragsmead had been futile in one sense, but at least he knew that he could not count on the Fitzwilliams to help him with Georgiana, which in turn strengthened his resolve to accomplish what needed to be done.

He took out a paper and began to write.

Reasons to marry:

Pemberley had been without a mistress too long.

Georgiana needed a married lady to chaperone her to balls and parties.

He needed an heir. He was not growing any younger.

A wife would lay to rest any feelings he may still harbor for Elizabeth Bennet.

Reasons not to marry:

He was in love with someone. Who despised him.

He tore up the list into tiny shreds and discarded them. The evidence was clear. There were plenty of reasons to marry and no reasons not to. He would have reason enough even if he were only doing it for Georgiana's sake. It was not as if he was performing a sacrifice by marrying, because there was no escaping the fact that his love was not reciprocated in any shape or form.

It was just his luck that he had to propose to the one person who could possibly turn him down. He could not think of one young lady he had met who would have done so.

He had been unlucky enough to fall in love with one of the least practical women in England.

He stared out of the window at the carpet of green extending in front of him. The gravel path leading down to the edge of the garden as it sloped down to the river. The bridge across the river. The valley running beside it. The hills beyond. And then, unseen from where he was standing, the fields and the tenants' stone cottages.

All these were his. They belonged to him.

Besides that, he came from an old and distinguished family, with an Earl as an uncle and other relations with titles.

Yet she had turned it all down without batting an eyelid, without even considering what it was she was refusing.

It was difficult to believe that such a blatant fortune hunter as Mrs. Bennet had produced such offspring.

Miss Elizabeth Bennet was as far from being a fortune hunter as she could possibly be. She had already proved that practical considerations mattered nothing to her when she had refused Mr. Collins. She had done it again by tossing his money, his property and his good name in his face.

So immoveable a dislike.

He winced at the words. He did not often meet people who actively disliked him. Perhaps he had spent too much time being surrounded by flatterers. Perhaps, like Lady Catherine, he was surrounded by people who fawned on him – Mr. Collins came to mind. Perhaps he was so puffed up with his own importance that he *expected* people to flatter him, and they did, which only made him puff up even more.

He shuddered at the idea.

The proof, though, was right before his eyes. He knew the truth. *He had not even considered the possibility that Elizabeth Bennet would turn him down.* Not for one second. He had been so eager to tell her about how unsuitable she was as a wife that he had never in his wildest imaginings considered that she might think him an even more unsuitable husband!

Of course, it was just as well Elizabeth Bennet had turned him down. He had thought of one more good reason why she was entirely the wrong person for him beyond the obvious ones he had explained to her at great length. A lady so indifferent to practical considerations could not be relied upon to run a house such as Pemberley, and the fact was, Elizabeth Bennet did not have a practical bone in her body.

Why, then, did he persist in this completely irrational obsession?

Enough.

He came to his feet and went to find Georgiana, to inform her that Lady Renwick and Miss Marshall would be coming.

~~X~~

Georgiana was excited to meet Lady Renwick and her niece.

She had never felt the absence of a mother as much as she had been feeling it lately. It vexed her that she knew so little about her neighbors. She had spent so little time here when she was away at school, and now there was no one to take her around and introduce her. Mrs. Annesley was a very agreeable companion, but she was not from around here and could not help her with the social rounds. Consequently, she had no friends here at all and few acquaintances beyond the tenants on their land and the poor to whom she dutifully took food and necessities at regular intervals.

She was sure the people in the village thought her proud. Little did they know that she would have loved to form some friendships in the village. Her friends from the academy lived so far away and she sometimes felt lonely. She wrote and received many letters, and her brother in particular was good enough to correspond with her regularly.

41

It helped, but she would still have liked to have friends close by. She knew some people in London, of course – the Bingleys for example – but because she was not out, this meant she was mostly restricted to a few families.

So when Darcy said he would be introducing her to a lady who was both their neighbor and a friend of their mother's, she was delighted. She was even happier when she heard she was to meet someone her age as well. She was determined to do everything in her power to make sure Miss Marshall became her particular friend,

Mrs. Annesley was sitting on a bench reading aloud from *The Absentee* by Maria Edgeworth while Georgiana was picking flowers in the rose garden when her brother stepped through the French doors, accompanied by two ladies. Georgiana supposed these were Lady Renwick and her niece.

She put down her flower basket and straightened out her dress.

"Do I look presentable, Mrs. Annesley?" she asked.

"You look very elegant," said Mrs. Annesley. "The blue pattern in your dress brings out the color of your eyes."

As they approached she smiled and greeted them as cordially as possible, making every effort to overcome her shyness.

"Georgiana," said Lady Renwick putting out her hands and grasping both Georgiana's in her own. "How grown up you have become! I can scarcely believe it! Let me look at you. I still remember when you were a baby clinging to your dear mother's apron strings. Of course, I saw you many times after that, but it has been a long time."

Georgiana glowed under Lady Renwick's gaze.

"Allow me to present my niece, Miss Elinor Marshall."

Georgiana gave a small curtsey.

Miss Marshall was very beautiful, with fashionable chestnut curls, light brown eyes, a little bud mouth and a great many little pink bows distributed all round her tall, dignified figure; bows on her trim, bows in her hair, bows on her sleeves and little bows decorating her bodice. She was also very self-assured.

"Miss Marshall has recently come down from London to visit her aunt," said Darcy.

"Will you be staying long, Miss Marshall?" said Georgiana, eager to start a conversation. From the corner of her eye she saw Mrs. Annesley nod approvingly.

"I hope to stay the whole summer."

"In that case, there will be time to further our acquaintance," said Darcy. "Meanwhile, I regret to say that I must leave you. Today is our first day of haymaking. I would like to be present in case any problems arise."

He bowed and took his leave.

Georgiana felt rather tongue-tied in the pretty brunette's presence, but she was determined not to allow that to hinder her.

"Welcome to our neighborhood, Miss Marshall. How do you find the country so far? Is it not beautiful around here?"

"No doubt it has its attractions, but I have always found the country a bore. It is good for two things only: hunting and house parties, and since I can attend neither, it leaves me with nothing to do." Miss Marshall had the kind of nasal voice that sounded commanding. "I had much rather be in Town. It will finally be my coming-out and I will be able to do so many things. Are you not looking forward to it as well, Miss Darcy?"

Georgiana was collecting her thoughts to answer when Miss Marshall continued.

"You will take well, for you are quite pretty, even if your hair is too light. I hear brunettes are all the rage." She gave her brown curls a shake. "'Tis a pity you do not have your brother's coloring."

"Come now, Elinor," said Lady Renwick, clucking gently and smiling at Georgiana. "Miss Darcy is exceedingly handsome and will undoubtedly soon have a long list of suitors vying for her hand." She leaned over and squeezed Georgiana's hand hard. "You are the image of your dear mama, who was considered quite the beauty in her day."

Georgiana blushed at the compliment. Then, as she noted the pale ivory of Miss Marshall's complexion, wished she wasn't so transparent. She would give anything to be like her brother, whose countenance

43

rarely revealed what he felt, but for some reason her feelings always seemed to be obvious to those around her.

"Fashions change, Aunt," remarked Miss Marshall. "It is quite different now from your time. Thank heavens! Just imagine you and I, Miss Darcy, having to wear patches and wigs!" She tittered at the idea.

"But that is all about fashion, not about beauty," replied her aunt, firmly. "Beauty is far more unchanging. A truly beautiful woman is beautiful no matter what the current trend may be."

Georgiana was grateful for Lady Renwick's defense, but having been in London in the Spring, she knew very well that brunettes were widely admired. She did not resent Miss Marshall for pointing out the fact. However, she did not like the way Miss Marshall was looking at her, almost as though she was assessing her as a rival. Georgiana squirmed uneasily under the close scrutiny; she felt as if Miss Marshall was trying to pry her open and discover her every thought.

"When do you plan to travel to London, Miss Darcy? I intend to arrive there as early as possible. I cannot *wait* to have a new wardrobe made. Who is to be your *modiste*, Miss Darcy?"

Georgiana tried to remember the name of the seamstress she had visited when last in London to have her new gowns made, but it had been someone she had never been to before, someone Miss Bingley had suggested. The name had slipped her mind.

"I—cannot recall," she said lamely. "Mrs. Annesley will know. She accompanied me there."

Mrs. Annesley opened her mouth to answer, but Lady Renwick waved her hand dismissively.

"Let us not talk about the Season just yet," intercepted Lady Renwick. "It is still several months away. Until then we must plan some diversions locally. I was intending to hold a small dance myself, to introduce my niece in Derbyshire, but it appears Mr. Darcy beat me to it."

"I hope we are still going to hold a dance at Houghton Park as well, Aunt," said Miss Marshall.

44

"Of course, Elinor. You shall have your dance. But first, we must assist Miss Darcy in organizing what will undoubtedly be her first large event."

"I will be grateful for any help you are prepared to give me, Lady Renwick," said Georgiana, "I am relieved to know I will not have to do it all alone."

Miss Marshall gave her a complacent smile.

"You may count on *both* of us, Miss Darcy. Fortunately, I have had the experience of helping mama with preparations for large events on numerous occasions. Your brother does not entertain often, then?"

Georgiana did not particularly care for the note of condescension in Miss Marshall's voice, but she told herself she was being too sensitive. It would be better to defer judgment rather than ruin what could be the beginning of a long-term friendship.

"My brother does not spend much time at Pemberley, and I was sent away to boarding school, so he was not in the general habit of hosting entertainments either here or in London. He does often invite friends to stay for shooting parties or fishing, however."

"Those are entirely different things," said Lady Renwick. "Bachelor affairs. You are old enough now to become a hostess in your own right. I am sure you will enjoy it."

Georgiana wished she could be as certain.

"We must set a date for the end of July," continued Lady Renwick. "Most local families will have retired to the country by then, and will be glad of some entertainment. We can expect the usual families to attend – the Greaves and the Batemans, for example – but we need to discover the new crop of debutantes and there may be families that have recently moved into the area. We also need to be careful not to slight anyone. I assume your brother is contemplating marriage, since he has asked me to produce a list of eligible females."

"I believe so," said Georgiana. "But I cannot speak for him."

She may have imagined it, but she sensed that Miss Marshall sat up straighter in her seat and looked suddenly less bored than she had while Lady Renwick was speaking.

"Very well," said Lady Renwick. "We will begin our campaign tomorrow. Before we start, we will have to pay a visit to Mrs. Parris."

She looked expectantly at Georgiana. "Do not tell me you don't know Mrs. Parris! Miss Darcy, you are very remiss in your duties!"

Georgiana instantly felt guilty.

"I am sorry—"

Lady Renwick laughed. "You need not look so downcast. I would not expect you to know her. She is our neighborhood gossip. She will tell you exactly what you wish to know. More than you need to know, in fact. I will signal to you if she starts speaking of anything inappropriate for young ladies' ears and you must promise me to cover them."

Georgiana could not help laughing. It was hard to believe that Lady Renwick had been in mourning for three years. She seemed so full of life.

She glanced over to Miss Marshall to share her laughter, but the young lady was looking disapproving.

"I hope you do not intend to introduce me to some vulgar nobody, Aunt. I have no interest in learning the latest provincial gossip.

Lady Renwick sighed. "Never underestimate the importance of gossip, Elinor. It has the power to both elevate and destroy young ladies such as yourself."

Miss Marshall raised her chin. "You need not remind me, Aunt. I would never give the gossips occasion to say anything about me."

Georgiana could not help but feel resentful about such a remark, particularly since she knew how perilously close she had come to being fodder for the gossips herself.

For the first time, she considered what it would be like if her brother were to marry. What if he chose someone like Miss Marshall?

She dismissed the idea as quickly as she thought of it. She had nothing to worry about. Her brother would never so much as glance at someone like Miss Marshall.

Chapter Six

Darcy took off his top hat to cool his head and fanned himself with it as he surveyed the fields with satisfaction. It was the ninth of July, the second day of the harvest, and already the field hands had made more progress than he could possibly have hoped. The weather was holding – the cloudless blue sky making the conditions ideal, though his sympathy went to those who were toiling under the summer sun. The haymakers were making the best of it while it lasted, however. No one knew when the weather would turn. Old Tom Able was predicting a few more days of sunshine – based on his rheumatic joints – so perhaps they would be lucky enough to finish mowing before rain came in.

The ninth of July. It was now precisely three months since the unfortunate encounter between him and Miss Bennet. He wondered – not for the first time – if he should have given that letter to Elizabeth. At the beginning, he had wanted desperately to ride off to Meryton to find a way to talk to her. Only a will of iron had held him back. That and the knowledge that he had embarrassed himself beyond redemption. He still could scarcely believe that he had approached the whole incident in such a heavy-handed manner.

As if the initial proposal wasn't arrogant and insensitive enough. He had then gone on to make matters worse.

I might as well inquire why with so evident a design of offending and insulting me, you chose to tell me that you liked me against your will, against your reason, and even against your character?

Could you expect me to rejoice in the inferiority of your connections?— to congratulate myself on the hope of relations, whose condition in life is so decidedly beneath my own?

No wonder she had accused him of not being a gentleman.

Your selfish disdain for the feelings of others.

Try as he could, he could not get those words out of his mind.

A commotion in the field drew his attention. The haymakers had stopped working and were all gathering in one place. Darcy sped his horse towards them, dreading what he would find. Every year there was at least one accident in which a scythe slipped and injured one of the haymakers. Last year a man had died of lockjaw from a large cut on his hand. One year a woman had almost bled to death when a neighboring scythe had cut open her thigh. Luckily, the surgeon had arrived in time to stitch the wound and stop the bleeding.

Driven by a sense of urgency, he slid off his horse and began to run, taking off his coat and waistcoat as he moved. They would need a clean cloth to tie the wound, and his shirt was likely the cleanest among them.

The haymakers parted as he approached. A young lad of twelve was sitting on the ground, crying, holding a bloodied hand.

"We need to bind the wound," said Darcy, urgently.

A woman who was standing beside the boy shook her head.

"'Tis nothing but a shallow wound, Mr. Darcy," she said. "Nawt to bother your head about. He's just a big blubbering baby, that's all. *And* he wanted to use it as an excuse for a rest."

There was some good natured laughter and the workers began to move away.

"Still, he isn't likely to be able to do much work with that hand, is he?" said Darcy. He tore a strip from his shirt and bound the wound while the boy looked sullenly at the ground, angry at his mother for exposing him like that in front of the master.

"He doesn't have much choice," said the mother, roughly. "We're hired labor. We get paid by how much we bring in at the end of the day."

"What's your name, lad?"

"Jimmy Dixon, sir."

"Well, then, Jimmy. Give me the scythe," he said. "I will do some of the work. Let's give the wound a chance to stop bleeding, at least until we discover if I need to call the surgeon to stitch it up."

"Oh no, Mr. Darcy, you can't do that," said the woman, horrified. "You'll spoil your hands. Come on, Jimmy. You can't let Mr. Darcy do your work."

The boy reached out to take the scythe from him, but Darcy waved him away.

"Leave it for now, lad," said Darcy. "It won't kill me to do a bit of work."

It would probably do him a world of good. It would be good to spoil his hands, to have them blistered and raw. It would distract him from that other pain. He could lose himself in physical labor.

But an hour later, under the burning sun, he felt that it *would* kill him. Bending over double was not something he was accustomed to. He had thought his fencing practice would come in handy when reaping, but fencing with a straight back was a completely different animal from this constant twisting and bending and careful hacking. His back was so painful it felt as if he would never be able to stand up straight again. Even though he'd long ago dispensed with his cravat and his shirt was open and torn, he was dripping with perspiration.

He forced himself to continue, however. It was a matter of pride to prove that he could.

~~x~~

As the carriage carried them from Mrs. Parris' house back towards Pemberley, Lady Renwick was looking very pleased with herself.

"What do you think, girls? Would you not name our visit a success?"

Georgiana's ears were ringing with all the information she had been exposed to. Mrs. Parris was fond of reporting the latest scandals, and Lady Renwick had been forced to interrupt her on a number of occasions to remind her that there were unmarried ladies present. This did not prevent Mrs. Parris, however, from revealing a few salacious nuggets.

They had certainly brought a blush to Georgiana's face. Georgiana had found herself giggling in a particularly silly manner, uncertain how to react to one particularly suggestive tale she heard.

Miss Marshall, however, had sat ram upright throughout, her face impassive, pretending not to have heard anything. Or perhaps she really was not listening.

She was sitting ram upright now, too. Georgiana was finding it harder and harder to like her.

49

Lady Renwick, however, was proving to be far more agreeable than she had expected.

"My head is in a whirl," she confessed to Lady Renwick. "Though I will confess that Mrs. Parris proved to be very useful, as you predicated. She has certainly supplied me with names of people to invite, and those I should categorically not invite, but without writing them down I am not sure I will remember any of it."

"From what I could gather," Miss Marshall declared, proving that she *had* been listening after all, "there are only a handful of families whose acquaintance I would consider worth pursuing. It will be easy to recollect who they are."

"You need not worry, Georgiana," replied Lady Renwick, kindly. "I know many of the people she was talking about. I merely needed to hear the latest *on-dits* to discover what changes have happened since— since I went into mourning. I have been away for three years, you know, and a few things have occurred in my absence, but not as much as I would have expected." Her eyes twinkled. "Not as much as I would have *liked*."

"Mama considers gossip vulgar," said Miss Marshall.

"Well I do not," said Lady Renwick, firmly. "Particularly in this instance when we are in need of information. I have emerged with a list of nine potential candidates I would recommend inviting, subject of course to Mr. Darcy's approval. I would call that a good day's work."

Miss Marshall looked unconvinced, but did not continue the discussion. No doubt she thought it vulgar to argue.

The afternoon was hot, and the heat was even worse in the enclosed space of the carriage.

"May I let down the window?" asked Georgiana, reaching for sash to pull it down. "The air outside may be a little cooler."

"Certainly not," said Miss Marshall. "The breeze will toss our hair and ribbons about. I dislike looking disheveled, even in the country where no one will know us."

Since there was not the slightest breath of air outside, Georgiana could not imagine that the small breeze that came from the movement of the carriage would make much of a difference. They were moving quite sedately, in any case. She was rapidly reaching the conclusion that Miss Marshall was overly careful about her appearance.

The carriage passed by a group of laborers who were cutting hay. Georgiana felt sorry for them, having to work in this heat. Their faces were reddened by the sun and the men's shirts were soaked through, clinging to their bodies.

It was unladylike to stare at the hard muscular bodies outlined by the wet shirts, but Georgiana could not help it. Her gaze was drawn irresistibly towards them. She felt a flush of warmth run through her.

Confused, she was about to look away when she spotted someone she recognized.

"Oh, look," said Georgiana, "there is Darcy!"

Miss Marshall turned away from the window, her sharp aristocratic nose rising in disdain.

"Do you not think men are more akin to beasts than ladies are, Miss Darcy? I find perspiration appropriate for horses or pigs but not for persons. I have heard – and I have come to believe it – that an infallible test of a gentleman's refinement is how little he sweats."

Georgiana eyed Miss Marshall's perfectly cool demeanor. There was not even a hint of moisture on her face despite the heat in the carriage. Georgiana became intensely conscious of that fact that she herself was wilting, and wondered if she ought to take out her kerchief from her reticule and wipe away any traces of dampness from her face and neck, or whether she had already been judged to be unrefined and she was already beyond redemption.

At least she was not alone in that. In the other corner of the carriage, Mrs. Renwick was fanning herself continuously. There were beads of moisture on her brow and her curls were plastered to her face and neck.

"Does your brother often work in the fields?"

The note of censure in Miss Marshall's question was obvious.

"Not usually," said Georgiana, "I daresay he had good reason for it. Perhaps they are expecting rain tomorrow and need to bring in the hay quickly."

She did not know much about fields or crops or agriculture, but she knew a little about haymaking. She had always loved the haymaking season. When she was a young child she had often ridden on the haystacks as they were carted away to be baled. Consequently, she had overheard countless conversations on the subject.

"Do you not find it uncouth to have him, a gentleman, doing manual labor there without a coat, his shirt open like a farmhand, smelling of sweat and hay?"

"He does not make a habit of it, but perhaps it encourages the laborers to see their master working amongst them."

She tried not to take offense at Miss Marshall's questions. After all, if Miss Marshall had lived much of her life in town, she did not understand the importance of agriculture in the running of Pemberley. Besides, even *she* had been surprised to see her brother, usually such a fine model of propriety, in such a state of undress.

"This is why men require wives," said Miss Marshall. "They need a feminine influence to help them overcome their base nature."

"For a young lady of such tender sensibilities as you, Elinor, it is naturally shocking to see a gentleman dressed in such a manner, but at the expense of sounding outrageous, I will admit I found Mr. Darcy a rather welcome sight."

Miss Marshall looked embarrassed at her aunt's statement. Georgiana was torn between blushing and laughing. She was coming to realize that Lady Renwick was not quite the decorous companion Georgiana had expected when Darcy had introduced her.

"Stop the carriage," ordered Lady Renwick.

"You cannot mean to have him ride with us, surely," said Miss Marshall in horror, abandoning her self-possession and pulling at her skirts as if afraid to have them contaminated.

"Of course not," said Lady Renwick. "But I thought he might wish to join us for luncheon. Will you ask him, Georgiana?"

Georgiana did not know what to do. She did not want to embarrass Miss Marshall, and she wondered if stopping the carriage would cause her brother embarrassment as well. But it was too late. She did not want to counter Lady Renwick's command, and they had already come to a halt.

She tried to repair the damage the best way she could think of by opening the window instead of the door, and leaning out to block him from the gaze of Miss Marshall.

As Darcy looked up and spotted the carriage, he scrambled to find his waistcoat and coat and to put them on.

"Are you coming back for refreshments, brother? We were just returning home."

"I would welcome a mug of ale and some cold meats. This is hot work," said Darcy.

"Then we shall wait for you."

He nodded "I will follow on horseback."

He turned away. Georgiana signaled for the carriage to continue.

It was very clear from the sour expression on Miss Marshall's face that she found the whole thing distasteful.

Georgiana felt bitterly disappointed. She had hoped to forge a new friendship with Miss Marshall and perhaps even to have someone with whom she could share her Season, as Lady Renwick and her mother had done.

But the gap between them only seemed to be widening.

~~X~~

Darcy had never been more grateful for an interruption in his life. At least now he had an excuse to leave while he could still walk.

He handed the scythe over to Jimmy along with a threepenny coin.

"Make sure you get your mother some good food on the table, do you hear?"

The look of joyful astonishment on the boy's face more than made up for the burning pain in his muscles.

He was spending too much time in town. He needed to spend more time on the estate, overseeing the work and getting to know his workers.

Yet another reason it was time he found himself a wife and settled down.

As he rode back to Pemberley, he considered the matter seriously. Would someone like Miss Marshall fit the bill? What was it exactly he was looking for? She had the right background. Lady Renwick was the daughter of an Earl, like his mother had been, and their family was old and respected. He knew very little about Miss Marshall's father other than the fact that he was a member of White's, which at least indicated that he was well connected. Darcy could write and make a few discreet enquiries, of course. She was pretty enough, too, and from the little he had seen of her, she seemed quite capable -- not a shrinking wallflower, certainly, which would not do at all for an estate like Pemberley. She did not seem the type to harbor romantic notions, either. She was elegant and well-mannered and undoubtedly had the usual accomplishments of young ladies.

If he had to get married – and he clearly did, since there was no point in prolonging his suffering over Elizabeth Bennet when she would not have him – then one bride was as good as another.

Miss Marshall was close at hand. Unless she was holding off for a title, he was an attractive enough prospect. He could save himself a great deal of time and trouble if he were to propose to her.

It was all perfectly logical.

His heart protested, but he was having none of it. His heart had no say in the matter. Consulting his heart in the matter of marriage was a foolish indulgence, nothing more. Men fell in love and out of love all the time. It was a passion of the moment, forgotten soon enough. Marriage was about producing heirs and managing a household. It was the choice of a lifetime.

He could not help feeling that a lifetime was a very long time.

Darcy rang for his valet as he entered his chamber and ordered warm water sent up for him to wash. It would not do to appear in front of his possible future bride smelling of labor and the fields. A glance in the mirror revealed that his appearance was even worse than he had thought.

In addition to his clinging, sweat-soaked shirt, there were bits of hay in his hair. He plucked them out one by one, forcing himself to be patient, curbing the sense of restlessness that told him he did not care how he appeared to anyone.

It was precisely this kind of impulsive behavior that had led him into trouble with Miss Bennet. He could not remember now exactly what had propelled him to take his coat off and start working, but he should have remembered that Georgiana would be returning that way with Miss Marshall and would very likely see him.

The last thing he wanted to do was to frighten off Miss Marshall by appearing boorish. Unlike Miss Bennet, Miss Marshall would not derive any amusement from seeing him covered in hay. He had the impression that she was a serious and meticulous type of person, which was precisely the type of wife he needed to run a large household like Pemberley.

The little valet entered with a jug of warm water and proceeded to pour it into the china basin.

"What clothes shall I lay out for you, sir?" said Briggs.

"My gold and navy waistcoat and my superfine navy coat."

Briggs looked surprised.

"Isn't that a trifle formal for this time of day, Mr. Darcy?"

Darcy gave the old retainer a faint smile.

"You've caught me out, Briggs. I wish to make a good impression on a certain young lady."

The little valet smiled broadly.

"I thought so. If you don't mind my saying so, sir, this is very good news. Very good news indeed. The house has been without a proper mistress far too long. Not that Miss Darcy isn't doing her best, of course. But it isn't the same as having a proper mistress."

"Don't you go spreading rumors downstairs, now," said Darcy. "I have only just begun the process of searching for an appropriate young lady. As you say, finding the right mistress for Pemberley requires careful thought. It will not be an easy task. Nor would I wish it to be. I

intend to take my time making my choice. So say nothing of the matter at this point, please."

"As you wish, Mr. Darcy. But you won't be able to stop speculation, if you don't mind my saying so. Not if you go downstairs dressed formally for a mere luncheon."

As Briggs helped him on with the tight navy jacket he surveyed himself in the mirror. He had lost some weight. The jacket, which had fit him like a glove, now hung a little loose. There were dark circles under his eyes that not even the best clothing could hide.

The familiar sense of dissatisfaction resurfaced. What was it he had said at the Meryton Assembly on that fateful day? He had told Sir Walter that every savage would dance. It had come out wrong, of course. The words had tripped out and acquired a different meaning. He did not mean to imply that those who were dancing at the Assembly were savages. He meant to say that the trappings of civilization could not hide the fact that underneath, all humans were savages at heart. It had been meant to be a witty philosophical observation. Instead, it had come out as a sneering statement of superiority.

It was those trappings that he was depending on right now. Briggs was surprised that he wished to appear so formal. What he could not tell Briggs was that he needed the clothes desperately to remind himself of who he was.

Somehow he had lost his way – he no longer recognized who he was. By giving in to his passion for Miss Bennet, he had laid aside all the parameters that defined his identity. It was like opening the floodgates. His passion had swept him along like a tide, and he no longer recognized the person he saw in the mirror.

By wearing these clothes – the starched cravat, the high pointed collar, the tight coat, he was assuming the trappings of civilization again. If he could not recognize who he was any longer, at least externally he could retain the same image he had always had. Later in the afternoon, he would send for his tailor and have the coat refitted to take into account the weight he had lost.

Meanwhile, he would impress upon Miss Marshall, and any of the other young ladies he would encounter, the importance of his status and necessity of finding a young woman who would be worthy of taking over the running of Pemberley. He regretted the fact that he had been seen half-undressed, working in the fields.

He had allowed Miss Bennet's teasing and her laughing eyes to pierce his guard, and what a mistake that had proven to be! He had laid his feelings bare to her and she had trampled all over them. Then, to add insult to injury, she had accused him of not being a gentleman. The irony of it! When he had abandoned all pretense for her sake!

Well, it would not happen again. From now on, he would be the perfect gentleman. No one would ever know that once upon a time, he had allowed the mask to slip.

Chapter Seven

When Darcy walked into the drawing room, he looked so formidably stiff that Georgiana wondered if she had imagined seeing him working in the fields in a state of half-undress. The transformation was complete. She hardly recognized this austere gentleman with cold grey eyes and starched shirt collar reaching halfway up his cheeks. For the first time ever, she noticed he resembled their aunt, Lady Catherine, particularly since his collar hindered his movements and forced him to look down his nose at all of them.

He did not say a word, either. He simply stood at the entrance of the drawing room, looking as though he'd rather be anywhere else than here. She wished now she hadn't stopped the carriage to ask him to join them.

To cover up for his unusual lack of civility, Georgiana went across the room to him and smiled broadly.

"I'm so happy you could join us, Brother," she said, slipping her arm through his. "You will be happy to know we have the beginnings of a guest list already. Lady Renwick's help has been invaluable. Would you like to look over the list while I ring for food?"

She was surprised at herself. Not only did she sound very self-assured but she was actually helping her brother out in a social situation. This was so unprecedented that she could hardly believe it was happening.

When Darcy did not say anything, her uncertainty returned. Suppose she was doing the wrong thing? What if Darcy snubbed her and made her look foolish?

"I certainly intend to look over the list, Georgiana," he said, giving her a tight smile. "We have to make sure not to invite anyone objectionable."

He almost sounded like Miss Marshall. What had come over her brother? Why this stiffness? Why the sudden insistence on correctness?

"No doubt you know some of people on the list better than I do, particularly since I have been – indisposed for so long," said Lady Renwick. "One can never know everything in any case. There's a rascal in even the best families – someone who can charm people out of house and home and is almost impossible to detect."

Wickham. Lady Renwick was speaking of Wickham. But then Wickham wasn't actually part of their family.

"I agree with Mr. Darcy," said Miss Marshall. "One cannot be too careful about these things. There are always men who take advantage of the unwary – and there are always ladies who are silly enough to believe them. Vigilance is the key."

Georgiana bristled. *I'd like to see you resist someone as handsome and charming as Wickham.*

But then, she supposed, a superior person like Miss Marshall would never even go anywhere near Wickham, who was merely a steward's son and not worthy of her interest.

If people knew that Georgiana had been on the verge of eloping, and with the steward's son, no less —

Her face grew hot with embarrassment. She had almost succumbed to Wickham's persuasions, and what a scandal that would have been! Her only excuse was that she was very young, and had been lonely and left too long with a companion who had deliberately misled her. Wickham had flattered her and made her feel – special. Attractive and special.

When they reached the sofa, Darcy withdrew his arm from hers and after waiting for her to sit down, arranged the tail of his coat and sat down, bending one leg and keeping the other straight, striking up an aristocratic pose as if he was about to have his portrait drawn.

Georgiana realized she was gawping at him and turned away quickly to ring for the cold cuts.

Her gaze landed on Miss Marshall. There was a speculating look on her face.

Oh dear. Was her brother being like this because he was trying to impress Miss Marshall?

It was not a happy thought.

~~X~~

Darcy was finding it difficult to breath. Sweat was trickling down under his collar. Of course it was an exceedingly warm day. His time in the sun had exposed him to the heat. On top of it, Briggs had tied his cravat too closely.

It was like a noose around his neck.

Darcy examined Miss Marshall surreptitiously from time to time while she ate. She took small, dainty bites, careful not to open her mouth too wide, almost as if she did not wish anyone to see her teeth. Darcy found himself watching her, trying to catch a glimpse of what she was so determined to hide. Did she have something wrong with her teeth?

One could tell a great deal about a horse from its teeth. It was perhaps a very cold approach to things, but he felt further knowledge of Miss Marshall's teeth might be important at this point.

The more Miss Marshall endeavored to hide her teeth, the more determined Darcy was to discover whether she was concealing something.

He was so intent on considering this possibility he did not realize that Lady Renwick was watching him speculatively.

"I beg your pardon," he said. "I'm afraid I was wool-gathering."

Lady Renwick threw her niece an indulgent glance. "I can quite understand the direction of your thoughts, Mr. Darcy," she murmured.

Why could a gentleman not so much as glance at a lady without the whole world assuming he was on the verge of offering for her?

"I rather think not, Lady Renwick," he said. And a good thing too.

He felt guilty for even thinking of Miss Marshall's teeth. She was a pretty, well behaved young lady, far too young to have problems with her teeth. Clearly, he was trying to find fault with her.

The way he had found fault with Elizabeth Bennet initially.

Not handsome enough to tempt me.

Must she intrude even now?

To dismiss her from his mind, he rose abruptly to his feet.

The upturned faces that looked at him expressed surprise. Seeing matters from their perspective, he realized he was behaving very badly indeed. If he continued in this manner, he would never find a suitable lady who would have him.

"I—" He searched around wildly for an excuse. "Do you not find it particularly hot today? I need to open the window."

He strode quickly to the window and, throwing it open, took in several breaths of calming air. He turned back once he was reasonably certain that he was in control of his emotions again.

Lady Renwick was again giving him a knowing look. It took him a moment to decipher what it meant.

Surely she did not think he was that perturbed by Miss Marshall's presence? He was not a lad of seventeen to behave in this manner when faced by a pretty face, especially when it belonged to a girl barely out of the schoolroom.

Worse still, Lady Renwick had seen his disturbance and come to the wrong conclusion. Give her a few minutes more and she would be planning wedding invitations.

"What we need to do," said Lady Renwick, cheerfully, "is set the date and issue the invitations."

Had he heard her right? Was she actually expressing her thoughts aloud? Was she already so sure he would offer for her niece?

"Do not you think it rather premature, madam?" he said, coldly, slipping his finger under his collar and trying to loosen the cravat a little.

She looked bewildered.

"Did you not say you wish to have the dance at the end of July, Mr. Darcy?"

The dance. Of course. She was referring to the dance, not to the wedding. He must be taking leave of his senses.

"Yes, of course. I had forgotten that we agreed on the date."

Miss Marshall was examining him gravely, an upright figure on the armchair, her hands neatly folded in her lap. She was judging him, no doubt, and finding him lacking in both wits and manners. He did not blame her. At the moment he was short of both.

"Are you planning to write the invitations yourself or are you comfortable having your sister do it?"

Lady Renwick was demanding his attention again. If he had known she would be so interfering, he would not have engaged her to help Georgiana. Did she really think he was going to go to the trouble of writing out a hundred or so invitations for a dance?

Georgiana would do it, naturally.

He threw a glance at his sister. She was looking nervous, as if she felt herself unequal to doing it. He felt guilty at once. After all, he had come up with the idea of this house party to find himself a wife. He could not expect his little sister to take on the whole burden of arranging it.

"We can share the task," he said, giving Georgiana an encouraging smile.

Her face brightened.

"At the last event my mother organized," said Miss Marshall, "I penned every invitation. There were one hundred and seventy five of them. My mother relies on me in such matters since she declares my penmanship is quite superior to hers."

She made the statement with such a dignified air of gravity that Darcy could not help but admire her. This was exactly the kind of mistress Pemberley required. She was poised, efficient and practical. He imagined her ten years from now, sitting in that very chair, completely unruffled at some crisis or the other.

Certainly she seemed unruffled at his erratic behavior. He had to give her credit for that.

"Your assistance must be invaluable to your mother," said Darcy, feeling called upon to make a gallant remark.

"I have three younger sisters, so as the eldest I am often in the position of responsibility. Mama has a great deal to take care of. She is forever arranging house parties and entertainments."

Darcy thought of Lizzy's younger sisters and made a mental note to find a way to meet Miss Marshall's siblings as soon as possible. One could tell a great deal about a family from younger siblings.

"You have no brothers?" he asked.

"None."

An awkward silence ensued. What should he say to that? I am sorry? Probably not, though of course, he was. It was always a problem to marry off so many young ladies in the same household. However, handsome dowries always made the task easier.

Mrs. Bennet did not have that luxury, which explained some of her desperation.

If Miss Bennet had agree to marry him, she would have saved her mother a great deal of anxiety. Did she not think of that?

"Well, then," said Lady Renwick, "Now that we have sorted some of the basics, we must take our leave. I must return to Sir Thomas. I do not want to stay away from him too long. He is accustomed to having me at home. I shall call on you again soon to discuss the arrangements with Georgiana. If she'll have me, that is."

"Of course," said Georgiana, eagerly, "I would be delighted if you could come. And Miss Marshall is welcome, too, of course."

"I look forward to seeing you both soon," said Darcy, bowing.

Miss Marshall gave a little bob of her head and glided regally from the room.

Darcy watched as the two ladies were handed into their carriage and drove away.

"She is very graceful, is she not?" remarked Darcy, turning to his sister.

"Miss Marshall?" said Georgiana, uncertainly, taking up a shirt she was making for him from her workbox and surveying her work. "If you say so. It seems to me she is perhaps a little stiff."

"Stiff? Is that not a little harsh?"

Georgiana put down her needlework and looked at him directly, lifting her chin. He recognized it as a gesture she had used as a child when she was being defiant. "It is not harsh at all. From what I have seen of her, in fact, I cannot help but feel she is very unbending."

It was unusual for Georgiana to state her opinion so firmly and on such short acquaintance. Still, if there was any possibility of him marrying Miss Marshall – and he had not yet made his mind up about It – he did not want to encourage Georgiana in her dislike.

"Miss Marshall is a serious-minded young lady. She comes from a titled family and is conscious of her position in society."

Georgiana twisted her hands together in her lap. "I— I do not believe her capable of deep affection, Brother."

Darcy looked at his sister in surprise.

"You have known her for no more than two days. She has not yet warmed enough to you to unbend. I am sure further acquaintance will prove otherwise."

Georgiana did not look convinced.

"Georgiana, you must understand that choosing a bride for me must consider a great many things, and that affection is only a minor requirement in a long list that includes more important prerequisites."

"You cannot convince me you believe that, Darcy," she said. "Only two days ago you were against my uncle's concept of marriage. Now you are suddenly advocating it?"

She had called him Darcy. It was the first time as far as he remembered that she had done so. It put a distance between them. It revealed the extent of her disillusion.

So be it. Sometimes a gentleman had to accomplish what he had to accomplish.

"Perhaps there is some wisdom to the way our predecessors did things. We cannot afford to indulge ourselves, not with grand estates to run and peoples' livelihoods at stake."

He looked away from the bitter disappointment in her eyes. He didn't blame her. He was stripping her of fairy-tales and baring reality before her. He too had been stripped of them. He had learned the lesson the hard way.

He had lived in heaven once – had felt there was more to life than the restricted world of proprieties and manners that had been bred into his very bones. He'd been willing to set aside those things – his status in society, the nobility of his family name, the approval of his relations – everything, in fact, that was important, for the sake of love.

He was not the first, nor the last to fall under the spell of love. It was an old story – and a stale one. How many people in history had destroyed their lives forever under the destructive power of love?

Fortunately, Elizabeth Bennet had not wanted him. She had saved him from his own folly. She had been wiser than he, knowing they belonged to different spheres, that they belonged to different social circles.

Then he remembered. Georgiana had been through this as well.

Both of them had loved, and both of them had failed in the objects of their love. Georgiana had been compelled to put Wickham behind her, too.

Now that he understood the suffering she had been through, he wished he'd been around her more to lend her support.

He sighed.

"Let us not discuss Miss Marshall," he said. "It's too early in the game. I am currently compiling a list of the qualities I am looking for in a wife. We shall see if they apply to Miss Marshall. Rest assured that I will not be swayed by a pretty face. I will be choosing carefully and rationally."

"I see," said Georgiana, in a strained voice. "I hope you plan to consult with someone at least before making a decision."

His first reaction was anger. It was not up to Georgiana to point out what he should or should not do. It was no concern of hers.

The anger dissipated almost immediately. It *was* very much her concern. Georgiana was the only living member of his family. Any wife he chose would have a huge impact on her life. With a sudden insight he understood that a wife of his could threaten Georgiana's happiness and could even come between them.

She was looking down at the ground in front of her, her face desolate. A fierce protectiveness rose up inside him. His heart went out to her. He was not only a brother to her but a father and a mother, too. Surely she was entitled to have some say in choosing his wife? It was important for Georgiana to like his new wife; he did not want to make her miserable. She had already had little enough happiness in her life. He did not want to lose his little sister.

He would have to select someone who would be kind to Georgiana. Another requirement he would have to place on his list.

Choosing a wife would take more careful thought than he had imagined. Already the mental list was growing longer by the minute. He should write it all down.

He stepped over to his sister and took up her hand. It was small and delicate against his. "I won't do anything foolish, I promise," he said. "I do want you to approve of my choice."

When she raised her gaze towards him, her lashes sparkled with tears, but her eyes were bright with happiness. Jumping up, she threw her arms around him, as she used to when she was younger, burrowing her nose into the hollow beneath his shoulder.

"You're the best brother in the world," she said.

He only hoped he'd be able to live up to her expectations.

Chapter Eight

When he was at Pemberley Darcy generally liked to start the day with a long ride, then a read through his correspondence. Rather than leaving it to his steward to sift through the letters, he did so himself. He trusted his steward implicitly, but when he was in residence he preferred to oversee matters himself. It was his way of keeping in touch with the business of the estate – it gave him a clearer idea of how well the estate was doing as well as its expenditure.

So far everything he had opened had been business related. Unless they required particular action, Darcy set those aside in a wooden box for his steward to answer.

The next letter he picked up was in an unfamiliar hand, but he recognized the seal at once. The Earl of Matlock. It was not the Earl who had written, however. The letter was from Lady Matlock.

Dear Nephew,
Since your unexpected visit, Lord Matlock and I have not been idle. As promised, we have embarked on a search for a suitable husband for Georgiana. Naturally, as she is our niece, we intend to procure someone of impeccable breeding, which you will appreciate is not a task undertaken lightly.

To assist us in our endeavor, we plan to engage a reputable artist to draw a miniature of your sister. Indeed, we believe Richard Cosway, who as you know is official painter at Court, may be persuaded to do so as he was well acquainted with your uncle. We have written to him to engage him, and anticipate his response any day now. As soon as matters have been arranged, we will send him to you at Pemberley. Upon completion, he will bring us the miniature so we can begin our search in earnest.

I do not think we will encounter a great deal of difficulty. Both Georgiana's appearance and her fortune are in her favor. We have high expectations of her marriage.

Naturally we will do everything in our power to ensure that she is protected from unscrupulous scoundrels and fortune hunters.
Yours sincerely,

Your devoted Aunt

If only he had not thought of visiting them! He had gained nothing at all from the visit other than to draw their attention to Georgiana. And of all people, Richard Cosway, who was known as a libertine, was to stay at Pemberley? He could not think of anyone less suitable to be entrusted with the portrait of a young lady.

He would have to find a tactful way of undoing the damage and putting an end to their intervention before it led to embarrassment. Unfortunately, his uncle and his wife were not accustomed to being contradicted and would not take it at all well if he refused.

With a frustrated sigh, he put aside the letter. He would have to deal with it later.

There was no mistaking the handwriting on the next letter; the pointed, bold lettering was unquestionably Lady Catherine's.

His fingers trembled as he broke the seal. Memories flooded back of the last time he had been in Rosings. The vision of writing that letter to Elizabeth was so vivid it seemed almost like yesterday. He could smell the ink, hear the scratch of quill against paper, see the candle sputter as it burned down to the end and went out, leaving him in the dark. That moment was branded forever into his brain.

A letter he had never delivered.

He opened the letter in terror of what it should contain. What if his aunt wrote that Elizabeth had married someone else?

Ignoring everything else, Darcy skimmed through the two pages quickly. There was no mention of her name; or at least, he found none. Of course it was absurd to think that the letter could in any way be related to her. Her visit to Mrs. Collins had ended long ago. She was long gone from there.

Enormously relieved that she was not getting married, but deflating because there was no news from her, he took a deep breath to calm his rattling pulse and began to read Lady Catherine's letter.

It was dated from Rosings, two days ago.

Nephew -- It has come to my attention that you taking steps to arrange a marriage for my dear niece Georgiana and that somehow, inexplicably, my brother's wife Lady Matlock has come to be involved.

I must urge you to rethink Lady Matlock's involvement in this matter. Lady Matlock's circles, as you know, often include families intimate with her father, the late Viscount Henscott. I am certain you do not need me to remind you of the Viscount's unfortunate reputation and tendency towards gambling and I am equally certain you would not wish your sister to be associated with that set. The outcome could be nothing but trouble. On no account must you allow Lady Matlock any say in this matter.

My advice to you would be to write to Lady Matlock and dissuade her instantly from any interference in what is, after all, a matter of no concern to her.

Meanwhile, I am prepared to assist you in your endeavors myself. Even though I do not care to stay in Town for extended periods of time, particularly since Anne's health is so delicate, I feel it my duty to support you and my dear niece. Although I did not experience a Season myself, as I was married to Sir Lewis when I was very young, I flatter myself that I am an exceedingly good matchmaker. It takes a certain understanding of human nature to be able to find a compatible couple, and I am fortunate enough to be blessed with a great deal of understanding. Leave it all to me. Your sister will be in safe hands.

There is no news of any importance to convey to you from Hunsford. The Collinses were invited to dine at Rosings last Sunday. However, there were not enough of us to play whist so they departed early. Your cousin Fitzwilliam is too busy to pay us a visit, but has promised to do so when he has his next leave which is in a month's time.

Meanwhile, I would like to convey your cousin Anne's greetings. She would have written to you, but she is tired today and I do not wish to overburden her. However, rest assured that both she and I are awaiting your return to Rosings.

With fondness,
Your Aunt, Catherine de Bourgh

It seemed strange that his aunt had not mentioned Miss Bennet at all. Normally his aunt would have given him news of anyone he had encountered while he was at Rosings – she must have heard news of Meryton and the Bennets from Mr. Collins.

Was it possible that Lady Catherine had detected something objectionable in his attitude to Elizabeth?

His aunt was not the most perceptive of people, but she had the eyes of a hawk when it came to anything that had a bearing on his marriage to Anne.

A scratch on the library door alerted him to the fact that he had barely paid attention to its actual contents.

"Come in."

It was Georgiana.

"I have come to talk to you, Brother," she said, intently.

As she approached, her gaze fell upon the letter in his hand.

She wrinkled her nose. "I think I recognize Lady Catherine's hand, and the fact that you are scowling so heavily confirms it. What news of Lady Catherine and our cousin Anne?"

He contained his impulse to crush the letter and toss in a corner. Instead, he slid it towards the table to his sister.

"You may read the letter yourself. I believe it concerns you."

"Me? What can Lady Catherine have to say about me?"

"A great deal, as it turns out."

Georgiana skimmed through the letter and tossed it down with a groan.

"I suppose it is too much to hope that I may be allowed to fend for myself." She slouched in her chair and folded her arms across her chest.

"I fear, little Sister," said Darcy, amused at her reaction, "that you already have too many champions eager to take up your cause. You must decide, it seems, between Lady Matlock and Lady Catherine."

He passed Lady Matlock's letter to her as well.

She looked up as soon as she'd read it. "If I must choose, it must be Lady Catherine. That would be the lesser of the two evils. But there is no need to choose, is there, Brother?"

"No. However, as you can see, it makes it all the more imperative that I marry as soon as possible," he said, rising to his feet.

"Surely you do not plan to do so this very morning?" she asked, with a half-smile and a twinkle in her eye.

He could not help smiling in return.

"Not this morning, little Sister. But unfortunately I cannot delay very long."

"You do not have to put up with their interference, you know," she said. "You are a man – you can simply consign them to Hades if you choose."

"Where did you learn such language, I'd like to know?" said Darcy, mildly. "No, wait, I would rather not know."

"But it is true. I have no choice in the matter. I am merely a young unmarried woman, which gives everyone the right to determine my life, but you are free to reject them."

"It is not as simple as that. Granted, I have a great deal more freedom than you do, but as long as I do not have a wife who can undertake your launch into society, I fear they will continue to feel justified in interfering. A gentleman in my position is only free in as far as his freedom does not conflict with his duty. Duty must always take precedence, which is why marriage is more like a business transaction than a pleasure."

He hesitated. Last night as he had lain in bed, he had thought over what Georgiana had said and he had decided to involve her in his search. His pride rebelled against soliciting advice from a much younger sibling – one, moreover, who did not have a great deal of experience in the world – but asking her to help him compile a list of required qualities for a wife, after all, was nothing more than following certain social obligations. He could always add specific personal qualities later.

"If you are not doing anything particular this morning, I would appreciate your help in compiling a list of desirable qualities in a lady.

And if you choose, we could compile one for you – for your gentleman suitor."

The joyful astonishment on his face was enough reward.

"I was to have French practice this morning, but I am sure you will agree French is not as important as assisting you in selecting the essential qualities of a wife. I will inform Mrs. Annesley of my change of plans as quickly as I can, before you change your mind."

"I will not change my mind. You may take as long as you like."

"These days you are inclined to change your mind from one moment to the rest. I cannot depend on that," she said and ran laughing from the room.

~~X~~

"You are very giddy this morning, Georgiana," said Mrs. Annesley. "Is it the prospect of the dance that puts you into such high spirits?"

"Not at all. It is something else entirely. If I tell you, though, you must not mention it to anyone."

"You know I will never betray your confidence."

She knew Mrs. Annesley was trustworthy, but it wasn't really her secret to tell, so she felt a touch of guilt saying it. "I'm helping my brother compile a list of the most desirable qualities in a wife."

"Word is that he favors Miss Marshall."

Not if she could help it. She would do everything she could to dissuade him. She knew Miss Marshall was the path to unhappiness for her brother.

"Not if I have any say in the matter," said Georgiana.

"I see now why you are giddy. You are up to something."

Not up to something, precisely, but she felt a new sense of determination that she had never experienced before. It was the first time her brother had cared for her opinion. Someone actually valued what she had to say.

She knew she owed it to the change in her brother that had occurred lately. She had not liked the change in his character, but she was glad of this aspect of it at least.

She just hoped it would last.

A few minutes later, when she opened the door to the library, Darcy was not at his desk. A cursory glance round the room revealed that he was not there.

Could he have changed his mind already?

A sense of sick disappointment settled at the pit of her stomach.

She closed the door and began to walk slowly down the corridor. Well, it had been nice while it lasted.

As she was about to return upstairs to the schoolroom, the footman approached.

"Mr. Darcy says you will find him in the orangery, Miss Darcy."

The orangery. It was her childhood place of refuge, the place she ran to when she needed to be alone with her thoughts. Her private place. She liked the fact that he had chosen to see her there, but it did not sound very promising, not for making a list. There was no ink or paper in the orangery.

Still, at least he had not forgotten they were meeting.

As she entered the orangery, she took a deep breath, savoring the citrus scented air. She loved the bright yellow and orange dotted trees.

To her surprise, she found a card table had been set up, with ink and paper and a knife for sharpening the quill.

"This is an unusual place to set up a desk, Brother," said Georgiana, smiling.

His lips twitched. "I did not wish to do this in the library. I felt that a change in scenery might be more conducive to thought and it seemed to have worked, for I have already written three qualities I desire in a wife."

"I thought we were to consult on this."

"Naturally. You may approve or disapprove."

That was not exactly what she had had in mind. She fought a surge of disappointment.

He passed her the paper.

Qualities required in a wife:

Adequate musical ability with skill in singing and playing the pianoforte and preferably the harp as well.

An elegant, graceful figure.

Proficiency in painting, coloring screens and netting purses.

Georgiana's s disappointment increased with every line. As a list, it was severely lacking. Anyone who could write such a list did not have a romantic bone in his body.

"Well, Brother, that is a good beginning," she said carefully, not wanting to be critical and destroy the new and fragile bond between them, "but since it applies to the majority of young ladies I know, I cannot think it can be very useful."

It was not actually a good beginning at all. Was he trying to write a list that would ensure Miss Marshall stood a chance?

Darcy pushed his chair away from the desk and, leaning back, stretched out his legs. He looked curiously reluctant to proceed any further.

This was going to be harder than she had imagined.

She drew her own chair closer to the table, dipped the quill in ink, and crossed out the three items on the list.

Darcy watched her, an arrogant expression on his face.

She knew that stubborn expression. Well she could be very stubborn as well. She was not going to give up that easily. His very future was at stake.

"This is what I need from you," she said, firmly, though she quivered inside, astonished at her own daring. "If there is one quality, and one quality only, that you would require in your wife, what would it be?" she said.

Darcy shifted in his seat. He looked unhappy. In fact, he looked positively miserable. He abandoned the sprawl and leaned forward to place his elbows on the card table, propping his face between his hands.

"William, I do not believe it is such a difficult question. Surely you can think of one crucial quality you would like in a woman."

Darcy shifted again. He looked exceedingly uncomfortable. Was he in pain? She chided herself for not thinking of it. Of course, it must be the headache again.

"I'm sorry, Brother, are you in pain? Has the headache returned?"

"It is not the headache," he said, sounding surly.

It had to be the headache. What else would account for this sudden change of mood over a seemingly simple task? He had seemed perfectly cheerful a moment ago.

"Would you prefer to postpone the list until later?"

"No," he said. "We will work on the list now."

"Then tell me one quality that is important to you," she said, evenly.

"Very well, then. If you must have it," said Darcy, pushing the chair away abruptly and rising to his feet. "The most important quality for me in a lady is laughter."

And with that he strode away.

Chapter Nine

Darcy ran his fingers through his hair and glared at the confounded list that sat staring at him accusingly on his desk. Why was this so difficult? He forced himself to take up the ink pen and, bracing himself, wrote out the phrase.

A sense of humor.

Which was all very well, but he did not seem to be able to go beyond it. Nor was it the first time he had written the words. He glanced towards the overflowing waste paper basket. He had come up with many ideas, all of them inappropriate. The devil of it was that the list seemed to have a mind of its own. It was as if a magical being was taking control of his quill. On the last paper, he had written: *A confident, impertinent manner.* He would never have written the impertinent part. It was patently absurd. But the words were there and he had been forced to crumple up the paper and throw it with the rest.

Seeking help from Georgiana had not helped him. Quite the contrary. He had been doing well enough until she had challenged him to tell her what he really wanted. That had opened the floodgates, and now he didn't seem able to close them again.

Marriage had nothing to do with what he wanted. His desires, his *needs*, were irrelevant. It was about what was expected of him. His list, therefore, could only consist of requirements that would satisfy his position in society. A man in possession of a fortune was in need of a wife that could handle the responsibility it entailed.

He dipped his quill in ink and began writing again.

Forceful enough to command a host of servants in a large household.

That was certainly a suitable requirement, except that it conjured up the image of Lady Catherine, which was absolutely not the kind of woman he would like to have as a wife.

He scratched it out.

Georgiana's supposed intervention had helped in one way. His outburst yesterday had served the purpose of making him aware that he was not yet prepared to offer marriage to Miss Marshall or any other lady just yet. It was abundantly clear from his reaction to Georgiana's question that he had not quite set aside the past. A practical marriage was necessary, but could he do it so coldly-bloodedly, without any attachment at all?

Much as he hated to admit it, he needed advice. Until his unexpected attachment to Elizabeth Bennet, he had relied mostly on his own counsel, although he had spoken with his cousin the colonel from time to time about some particularly vexing issue, and of course he had consulted with him about anything to do with Georgiana. Even this much had not been easy, since the colonel was absent in the Peninsula for more than three years, but Darcy knew Fitzwilliam was reliable as well as a good friend. Still, Fitzwilliam had clearly been partial to Elizabeth when they were at Rosings, and had even expressed his regret that his limited income prevented him from paying her more attention. Consequently, Darcy did not feel comfortable discussing Miss Bennet with him.

He could, however, talk about marriage in general, he supposed. His cousin knew his taste in ladies; perhaps his cousin could even suggest someone Darcy might like.

Then there was Bingley, of course, his closest friend. Bingley had confided his attraction to Miss Jane Bennet from the first day he had met her. Darcy, on the other hand, had said little about Elizabeth Bennet. Part of it had been because he did not want to have to endure Caroline's prodding. She was altogether too sharp and mocking, and anything he said to Charles would be accidentally revealed to his sisters.

Bingley was a fine friend but he was not very good at keeping secrets.

He had certainly not spoken to Charles about Miss Bennet's rejection. It had all been too raw and humiliating. Darcy was afraid to admit that he had offered marriage to a woman without even ascertaining first if she would welcome his attentions. Even now he was overcome with embarrassment when he remembered how he had burst into the parlor at the Parsonage and without as much as a by-your-leave, had proceeded to propose, assuming she would be a fool not at accept him. He had not even practiced the proposal. He had blurted whatever came into his head, assuming at the time that the wording did not matter. Since he was bestowing a great honor on the Bennet family, she would be a fool not to grasp the opportunity he was offering. Since his father had died, countless ladies had vied for his attention. He'd simply assumed that, with Mrs. Bennet being as grasping as she was, her daughter was of the same mold.

He would never forget the expression of sheer astonishment on her face when he had started. And then – the emotions flitting across her face; confusion, mortification then injured pride followed by anger.

Had you behaved in a more gentlemanly manner…

Darcy had long since realized that, far from acting as a gentleman, he had behaved in the most condescending possible manner, never considering for a moment that she might reject him. He had been Lady Catherine at her worst, riding roughshod over everyone.

To think, that in Elizabeth Bennet's eyes, he had been no more tempting a prospect than that weak-headed clergyman!

Afterwards, he had not cared to admit to anyone that he had been such a buffoon, that he had bungled the whole thing so badly that Miss Bennet had felt no qualms in giving him a set down. He had turned and fled like a puppy with his tail between its legs.

Almost. Except that he had compounded his bad judgment by writing a letter to her, explaining at length the whole sorry story of Georgiana's botched elopement. Imagine if that letter were to fall into the wrong hands! He had been willing to sacrifice Georgiana's reputation in a last-ditch attempt to salvage his own.

Fortunately, he had never delivered it. At least he had had that much sense.

Naturally he had not talked to Charles about any of this.

He thought of Charles' face as he had last seen it. His friend had lost weight, and he had a haunted look to his face. Darcy felt the iron grip of guilt squeeze at him.

The man who has been the means of ruining, perhaps for ever, the happiness of a most beloved sister.

Charles and Jane. Two people rendered miserable by his arrogance and stupidity. Three if he included himself. And on top of everything else, he had driven a wedge between himself and Charles. He had quarreled with Charles before they came over some trivial matter. Charles had been in an uncharacteristically dark mood. And now, when Charles needed him, he had driven off to Pemberley and left his friend to his own devices.

A perfect solution offered itself. He usually invited the Bingleys and the Hursts to Pemberley in August, since until now, Bingley had not had an estate of his own to go to. Now Bingley had taken Netherfield but he could possibly go there for the hunting season.

He would write an invitation to them at once, asking them to join him and Georgiana. Now that Lady Renwick had taken care of who to invite, Caroline could help Georgiana plan the house party.

He could also ask the Bingleys for assistance in choosing a bride.

Darcy completed his letter to Charles with a sense of satisfaction. He had not said anything about his reasons for inviting them all to Pemberley. He had merely hinted that he required their assistance. He sealed the letter and turned with a sigh to answer Lady Matlock's letter.

Dear Lady Matlock,

Your interest in the matter of Georgiana's marriage is very much appreciated. However, I cannot allow you to take it upon yourselves to find my sister a husband. As her legal guardian, it is my duty to take care of her, especially in this matter, and I will do so when the time is appropriate. It is out of the question to marry her before she had been presented in Court and I will not consider any suitor until then.

In the matter of the miniature, I have no objection to having Georgiana's miniature painted. It would prefer another artist. However, if Richard Cosways has already accepted, please ensure that we are in residence in Pemberley before sending him here, however. It would be a pity for him to waste his journey.

He paused in his writing. He had to be careful. He did not wish to slight Richard Cosway, who was one of the best miniaturists in England. It really was not a bad idea to have someone draw a likeness of Georgiana now that she was fully grown; he just wished it did not have to be Cosway.

He put down the pen as a scratch on the door drew his attention. It was probably Georgiana, wishing to continue with the list. When the door opened, however, it was not Georgiana but Mrs. Reynolds.

"I am sorry, sir, but Cook wanted to know if there is something in particular you wish to have baked for tea. She is planning to make Georgiana's favorite – apple pie, but you must tell me what you would like served when Miss Marshall comes with her uncle and aunt."

Why would he want to serve anything in particular if their neighbors came for tea? Mrs. Reynolds rarely consulted him on matters of this kind. Why did she not talk to Georgiana?

There was an unusual expression on Mrs. Reynold's face.

He suddenly remembered his little valet. Apparently Briggs had wasted no time spreading word that he was considering marriage to Miss Marshall.

"I see," said Darcy. "You think I would like to impress Miss Marshall by offering her something she would particularly like."

"The thought did cross my mind, Mr. Darcy. I hope you do not consider it forward of me to mention it."

"Not at all, Mrs. Reynolds. But I want you to do something for me. I want you to discourage speculation. I am not discounting possibility, mind you, only since I am in the first stages of my search for a wife, I do not wish word to get out.

"I understand, Mr. Darcy." She turned to leave, then stopped and turned back to him. "Now that you have mentioned it, sir, I just wanted to tell you I'm sure your mother would have been very happy to know you are planning to settle down, sir."

He was touched by her consideration.

"Thank you, Mrs. Reynolds."

It was not only Georgiana who had a stake in whom he married. People like Mrs. Reynolds and the rest were depending on him to get it right.

"May I ask you a question, Mrs. Reynolds?"

She was at the door. She paused and turned back to look at him.

"Certainly, Mr. Darcy," she said, holding her hands together in front of her and waiting for the question.

"What do you think is the most important quality a wife worthy of Pemberley should have?"

"That is a hard question." She pursed her lips in thought. "There are so many possibilities."

"If you had to name only one?"

She gave a slight smile. "Then I would choose kindness, sir. Kindness is the most important quality the lady of the house must have. Most other things you can learn, but kindness isn't something you can pick up. You either have it or you don't."

"Thank you Mrs. Reynolds. That is very helpful. I shall put it on my list."

She was right, of course. He had not thought of that. As he wrote it down, pleased now that he had two items on his list, he considered that it was ironic how, in the one matter he expected to be entirely private, he seemed to need the most amount of help.

~~X~~

After the soul searching of the morning, the superficial conversation over tea was a relief. There was a certain comfort to be had in polite social conversation among equals. One did not have to invest too much in it either mentally or emotionally.

"Allow me to provide you with a tour of Pemberley, Miss Marshall. Mr. and Mrs. Renwick – I hope you will join us, even if you are already familiar with my home."

"I hope you will take my arm, Mr. Darcy, for I find the layout of Pemberley very confusing. It is set out so strangely I am sure one could wander around for hours and never find one's way."

"I assure you, Miss Marshall, once you are familiar with it, you will not lose your way."

"I sincerely hope I will have the opportunity to become familiar with it, Mr. Darcy," said Miss Marshall, giving a little laugh.

Darcy thought it rather forward of her to say so, but then he could hardly blame her. He had been the one who had brought up the idea.

There was something curiously formal about their little tea tour. It seemed staged, somehow, almost as if Darcy was trying to impress Miss Marshall with his wealth.

With Georgiana, Mr. and Mrs. Renwick and Mrs. Annesley following behind them, Darcy offered Miss Marshall his arm to escort her. Her arm felt birdlike in his, bony and wavering and altogether not quite solid, unlike Elizabeth Bennet's arm which was firm and warm. This arm seemed ready to slip out of his grasp any moment.

"Do you like the country, Mr. Darcy?" said Miss Marshall. "I find it has little to recommend it. The opportunities for social interaction are so limited."

Darcy remembered saying something similar about the country when he was in Netherfield, in Elizabeth's presence. Now he bristled at the idea that anyone would not wish to be in Derbyshire, or that his beloved Pemberley could be found lacking because of its location. No wonder Bingley had chided him and Mrs. Bennet had taken offence, though that did not make her remarks any less vulgar.

They paraded onwards through the hallway, advancing towards the Sculpture Room.

"This is a fine place you have here, Mr. Darcy, though it sadly lacks a woman's touch," said Miss Marshall.

That much was certainly true. He tried to see Pemberley through Miss Marshall's eyes. There were hints of shabbiness here and there – nothing obvious, just things that to a discerning eye would signal the absence of loving care. Yes, there were some changes that definitely needed to be made. He had kept up essential maintenance, that was all. He was glad Miss Marshall saw that. It was a promising beginning.

His hand twitched to add the latest quality to the list.

An ability to perceive what changes were needed for improvement.

"If you wish," said Miss Marshall. "I can assist Georgiana in selecting new material for the upholstery."

Darcy missed a step as he turned to look at his companion in surprise. *Now this was presuming too much too soon.*

"I rather think Georgiana would prefer to choose the upholstery herself, if I were to ask her to do it. However, I prefer to defer such changes until there is a mistress in Pemberley."

"Very wise of you, Mr. Darcy." Miss Marshall nodded her approval. "Whoever enters this house as its mistress will undoubtedly wish to instigate any number of changes. When one moves in the first circles, it would not do to appear shabby, and I expect the new Mrs. Darcy will wish to display the utmost refinement when she invites house guests."

Not planning to modify too many things in Pemberley. Another quality for the list. He hoped he would remember these qualities later on, when it came to writing them out. His hand went to his waistcoat pocket to feel for the outline of his list. Yes, it was still there, folded into tiny pieces to fit.

"Poor Georgiana lives such a secluded life while in Pemberley. I wonder what she finds to amuse her. There are not above half a dozen families that I would care to visit, and of those, several are insufferably dull. I believe living in the country blunts one's mind. Where is the stimulation of theatre, of the best circles of society, of museums with divine collections of paintings and sculpture?"

"Are you a connoisseur of art and sculpture, Miss Marshall?" he asked.

"Certainly. I adore Italianate art. Tortellini in particular."

"I'm unfamiliar with Tortellini's work," said Darcy, frowning in puzzlement. "However, if you are interested in Italian art, we do have a painting by Salvator Rosa which you might be interested in looking at, and one by Boltraffio."

They had reached the Sculpture Room. Darcy opened the double doorway leading into it, and bowed to his guests as they sauntered in. He was proud of the sculpture room especially the private collection of Greek statues. His father had been fortunate enough to acquire three statues from Lord Elgin which he had brought with him from Greece. He conducted his group to that collection immediately, knowing they would be impressed.

"You have a remarkable collection here, Mr. Darcy," said Mrs. Renwick. "A perfect combination of the old and the new."

"I echo your sentiments, madam," said Darcy. "The art collection, like the library, is the labor of generations. Each generation contributes something to it. I hope eventually to acquire something of my own to add to it."

"Well, those ones certainly look old," said Miss Marshall, pointing to the Greek collection.

"Yes," said Mr. Darcy. "Mr. Elgin brought them with him from Greece. They were rescued when the Parthenon was bombarded by the Ottomans."

"It is remarkable to think these statues were made so many centuries ago," said Mr. Renwick.

"It leaves one quite in awe to think of all the Greeks accomplished so many centuries ago," remarked Mrs. Renwick, "Mr. Darcy you are fortunate to have acquired such treasures."

Miss Marshall gave the statues a dismissive look. "Yes, but one might have hoped they would be in better shape. Instead, with a nose and an arm missing, they look positively grotesque. Not unlike Mr. Elgin himself, I believe. I have heard he lost his nose to some horrible skin disease, poor man. Perhaps he broke off their noses deliberately, to make them match his own." She tittered at her joke.

Darcy and Sir Thomas exchanged awkward glances over her head. It was well known in gentlemen's circles that Mr. Elgin's disease was in fact syphilis, something an unmarried lady would not be expected to know.

"I don't see why Mr. Elgin would have done such a thing," said Georgiana, looking rather vexed. "Marble statues such as these are subjected to the climate so it is a natural thing for them to be eroded."

Miss Marshall turned to Darcy, laying her hand on his shoulder. "*Eroded*? How droll! I did not imagine Georgiana to be such a bluestocking. What Academy for Ladies did you send her to, Mr. Darcy? I know, Georgiana, you have not been fortunate enough to have a mama to advise you, but you must know that a woman, if she has the misfortune of knowing anything, should conceal it as well as she could. If there is anything young men despise in a young lady, it is learning. She will not engage any gentleman if she exhibits her learning openly."

Darcy did not look at Georgiana, but he imagined her cowering under Miss Marshall's attack. He removed the gloved hand from his shoulder and tucked it firmly in the nook of his elbow. He would not permit anyone to attack his little sister.

"Not all gentlemen prefer ignorance in a woman," said Darcy. "Some may even prefer evidence of wit and quickness of mind."

He thought of Elizabeth Bennet and the way her eyes sparkled with intelligence.

Georgiana looked directly at Miss Marshall, "I am sure most gentlemen of your acquaintance, Miss Marshall, may prefer women who are uninformed young ladies," said Georgiana, "but I assure you I would not wish to marry such a man."

Darcy looked at Georgiana in surprise. Georgiana rarely contradicted anyone, yet here she was, showing her claws.

He held his breath. How would Miss Marshall react to the implied insult? She looked perfectly complacent, but he prepared himself to soothe some ruffled feathers.

"As mama would say, my dear Georgiana," she replied with an upward tilt of the chin, "we young ladies do not choose husbands. Our husbands choose *us*, and we must endeavor to find a way to attract them, like bees to a flower."

Darcy did not think Miss Marshall was doing a particularly good impression of being a flower, nor did he appreciate being cast in the role of a bee.

Another item for his list. Must not repeat her mother's words.

The list was coming along very well. Far better than he could have expected.

He tried to imagine what Elizabeth would have been like, if she had had an unfortunate tendency to quote Mrs. Bennet.

It did not bear thinking of.

Chapter Ten

"Why this sudden desire to go to Town, Brother? I thought you planned to stay in Pemberley for a while." Georgiana paused, wondering if it she would be incredibly rude if she mentioned a certain young lady, but she could not hold back. "This does not have anything to do with Miss Marshall and the fact that her mother has called her back to London, does it?"

Darcy gave his steed a nudge and rode up ahead of her.

Oh, dear. Now she *had* offended him. Georgiana sighed. It was so difficult to gauge what was right and what was wrong these days. It was all too easy to put her brother on the defensive.

Fortunately his reaction did not last long. Darcy soon slowed down and waited for her to catch up with him.

"Really, Georgiana, I don't know how you could think such a thing. I have many reasons to return to Town, among them the fact that I need to bring the Bingleys to Pemberley."

So now Darcy was to be the Bingleys' escort to Pemberley? What happened to corresponding through letters?

Darcy gave a small smile. "I see you do not think that reason enough."

Georgiana nodded. "I do not," she said stoutly. "I have rarely seen such a poor excuse."

Darcy's smile grew larger. "You're becoming quite outspoken, Georgiana. I can see that you have our Aunt Catherine's blood in your veins."

She recoiled at the idea. "It's no laughing matter, William Darcy. I'll have you know that I find the comparison odious." She gave a little shudder. "Heaven forbid!"

"Don't worry, little Sister, you still have a long way to go," said Darcy, laughing. "Not that I think it would be so very terrible. At least our Aunt has backbone."

"She's a veritable dragon," she replied.

"True," said Darcy, sobering suddenly, as if a painful memory had intruded.

Before he could sink into gloom again, Georgiana quickly diverted the conversation.

"You have not answered my question, William, and I won't be brushed off. Why exactly did you say you needed to go to London? And don't give me the Bingleys excuse because that's a bag of moonshine."

She felt quite daring, confronting her brother like this, but if Miss Marshall could do it and get away with it, then she had the right to do it as well. She was tired of being the quiet little mouse.

"Young ladies do not use cant expressions, Georgiana," said Darcy, raising his brow, but there was no real heat in his statement. "And it so happens that I have more than one good reason for travelling to London, and both reasons concern the Bingleys. The first is that I have quarreled with Charles, a quarrel, I should say, for which I am entirely to blame. I have invited him to join me in Pemberley and he has declined."

"Declined? Surely not, William? This is the first time I have ever heard you mention that you have quarreled with Mr. Bingley. He is so amiable it would take a great deal to make him angry."

"I dare say," said Darcy. "Nevertheless, I *have* managed to anger him. He did not even respond to my letter himself. Mrs. Hurst had to write and tell me. So now you know why I must pay penance by going to London to repair the damage."

Georgiana thought about this. It made sense, particularly if Bingley had refused to come to Pemberley. He and his sisters usually came to visit this time of the year.

"You said there was another reason?"

"I wish to ask the advice of Miss Bingley on finding a wife."

He was going to consult with Caroline? Of all people? Was he unaware that Caroline had her own ideas of whom Darcy should marry?

She would have thought that an infant in swaddling clothes would have noticed. She sighed. Perhaps what Mrs. Annesley said was true. Most people moved through life with blinkers on their eyes; they saw only what they wished to see and discarded anything that did not fit with their perception.

"But Darcy, do you think that is quite appropriate?"

"Why not? She is proficient at managing household matters. She was very proficient in setting up Bingley's new home at Netherfield. We scarcely felt the inconvenience of moving. She hired many members of the staff, though of course they brought their immediate staff with them, and set up the household in little more than a few days. She has a very practical mind and I am sure she will be able to advise me admirably. "

Except for one thing. Darcy seemed unwilling to acknowledge that there were other factors at play in this situation.

Well, Caroline Bingley could take care of herself. Though, come to think of it, Georgiana would not mind having Caroline as a sister. Caroline had her faults, not least of which was the way she tried to ingratiate herself with Darcy but at least there would be no surprises. Caroline had always given sound advice whenever Georgiana had asked her opinion, whether about clothing, household matters, or anything to do with music. She knew the Bingleys, knew what to expect.

Anything would be better than having Miss Marshall as her sister.

She could only hope that Caroline would find a way of distracting Darcy from Miss Marshall.

"It is true that Caroline's mind is of a practical bent," she said, realizing Darcy was waiting for her answer. "I am sure she will be very helpful in this matter. I just wish you weren't leaving again soon. I'm not quite ready to part company. I've hardly seen you."

"Who said we are to part company, my dear sister? On the contrary. I believe you need new clothes for the ball, and where better to have them made than in London? You and Mrs. Annesley are to accompany me. As long as you promise to help me mend my fences with Bingley."

Georgiana gave a whoop of joy. "Did I tell you that you are the best brother in the world?" said Georgiana. "I will promise you anything as long as you do not intend to leave me behind."

Here I come, Miss Marshall. You are not going to win this round, not if I'm around to prevent it.

~~X~~

The heat in London was unendurable. Darcy pulled at his cravat and longed for the open and fresh air of Derbyshire. The stench of rubbish and sewage rose from the streets in a haze, the dense buildings hemming in the heat and compounding it. No wonder the fashionable elite fled Town for the coast or the countryside.

The now-familiar specter of guilt rose up in Darcy as he thought of Bingley having to suffer the heat of London, knowing he had a country manor to go to, but unable to go to Netherfield because of Jane Bennet.

Well, he was going to help Bingley solve his problem. If both of them found wives reasonably quickly, Bingley would be able to go to Netherfield with his new bride, and everything would return to normal. The Bennets would no longer form a threat. If he could do it, Bingley could, too. There was no point in suffering when there was a clear solution to be found.

More than ever, Darcy was certain he had done the right thing in keeping Bingley from Miss Bennet. Bingley's position in society was far more tenuous than Darcy's. Despite his background in trade, Bingley had managed to find himself a place in elegant society. Granted, he had had Darcy's assistance, but he made friends easily and was so good natured no one could rebuff him. Marrying into a family of nobodys, however, would confirm his status as a hanger-on, and radically reduce his sister Caroline's chance of marrying well. Darcy would lose a little from marrying Elizabeth Bennet, but Bingley would very likely lose everything he and his family had striven for.

He had spoken to Caroline Bingley about this when they were in Netherfield and she had agreed that a hasty removal from Meryton was essential. A few months, they felt, would be all that was needed for Bingley to forget Jane Bennet ever existed.

Bingley was always falling in and out of love.

The fact that he had not forgotten yet did not bode well, but the worst was over. He would convince Charles to find himself a wife as well. Soon they would both be sensibly married and they would be able to put this nightmare behind them.

~~X~~

Georgiana barely had time to wash and change before Darcy was knocking on her door, urging her to hurry. She was finding it increasingly difficult to deal with her restless brother, all the more so since she had no comprehension of what was driving him. Was it possible he was madly in love with Miss Marshall? It seemed unlikely, but Georgiana did not pretend to understand the minds of men.

When they reached the Bingley townhouse, Darcy took the steps up two at a time. Naturally, he stood waiting impatiently as she walked up in a ladylike fashion. The Butler – Evans -- showed them in immediately. They found Caroline seated alone in the parlor. As he had anticipated, she was all astonishment to see Mr. Darcy.

"Mr. Darcy! What an unexpected pleasure. I wonder you did not inform me that you were coming to Town."

"I am sorry, Caroline, but my decision to come up was entirely unforeseen."

The astonishment quickly turned to speculation as she tried to ascertain the reason for Mr. Darcy's visit.

"Mr. Darcy, I was only just now determining which gowns I would need for Pemberley. I must admit to some surprise at seeing you here. I hope it does not indicate you have withdrawn your invitation. I was so looking forward to seeing Pemberley again."

"Not at all. As a matter of fact, I'm here to see Charles. He has turned my invitation down and I wish to know why."

"Surely you did not drive all the way to Town merely to speak to my brother," she said coyly. "I am inclined to think something entirely different brought you to Town."

"It so happens there was one other matter I wished to speak to you about, but first I must see Charles."

"Oh, Mr. Darcy! What could you possibly mean?"

"I hope you do not think me uncivil, Caroline, but I *must* speak to your brother."

"You'll find him upstairs. He has become such a bore. He sleeps half the day and mopes around the rest. You would hardly recognize him. If it were not for the fact that you expressly advised me not to do it, I would have told him to pursue Miss Bennet, if only to rouse him out of his dejection."

"Well, it is just as well I have arrived, then."

As soon as Darcy left the room, Caroline turned to her.

"Georgiana, you must tell me at once. What does your brother intend to consult me about? I am dying to know."

Georgiana had anticipated being asked by Caroline to reveal her brother's purpose. Since she knew all too well that Darcy had rekindled Caroline's hopes, she merely shook her head and pursed her lips.

"You must ask him yourself," said Georgiana, "I cannot speak for my brother."

But Caroline was not to be easily deterred.

"What could he have to say to my brother that is so urgent? Really, it cannot be about their quarrel. That happened weeks ago. There must be something else."

Georgiana shook her head. "I'm sure it has something to do with your brother refusing to come to Pemberley."

"Then why did Darcy say he has something particular to say to me?"

Georgiana winced. This was exactly what she had been afraid of. It was not her place to say something, but she could not allow Caroline to persist in her illusions.

"I believe he wished to consult you about something."

"Me? Darcy wishes to consult *me*? That is preposterous, Georgiana. Darcy never consults with anyone. No, it must be something else."

Yet another example of blinkers. How was it that people refused to see the truth when it was staring them in the face?

~~X~~

"For heaven's sake, leave me alone," said Bingley.

He was lying in his bed in a darkened room, the curtains drawn so that they would not admit any light. It was sweltering inside, the air so thick Darcy could hardly breathe.

Darcy found it shocking to see his normally cheerful friend in such a state. Oh, if only they had never taken Netherfield Hall, none of this would have happened! Why had he not had any premonition of disaster the day he had counseled Bingley to make a commitment?

He strode to the window, pulled open the curtains and let some air in.

"Get up, Charles. Enough wallowing in self-pity. Put on some clothes and let us go out in search of amusement."

"Oh, it is you, Darcy," said Charles, groaning. "I had rather hoped you had disappeared forever into the depths of Derbyshire."

Darcy pulled back the canopy of the bed and reached out to help his friend into a sitting position.

"Well, I have not, and what's more, I will not take no for an answer."

"No," said Charles, promptly, rolling over to his side and facing away from Darcy. "So there! I will have nothing further to do with you."

He sounded ridiculously childish.

"What, you have been sulking for three weeks because I refused to allow Caroline to inform you that Miss Bennet was in Town? Come now. Tell me you do not wish to throw away years of friendship over a woman you will have forgotten in a matter of weeks."

"I will not forget Miss Bennet. Assuming that is your biggest mistake, Darcy." Bingley turned to face him. "You know me. I am the best natured of men and very easily swayed, but conspiring with my sister to keep information from me deliberately? That is trespassing too far on my good nature."

"If we *had* revealed her presence, you would not have been able to stay away. You forget that we have dealt with a number of situations in which you declared yourself wildly in love. You are in and out of love constantly. In this case, we did not want to risk the possibility that you might ruin your life by offering Miss Bennet marriage on the spur of the moment."

Lord help him. That was precisely what he himself had done in the case of Elizabeth Bennet.

"I have told you repeatedly – this time it is different. I grant you that I am the most fickle of fellows when it comes to women, but my regard for Miss Bennet is unshakable. She is an angel, Darcy."

"An angel with a nightmare of a mother."

"I am not planning to marry her mother, as it so happens."

"Oh come on, Bingley. You cannot be so naïve as to imagine you will have a moment's peace if you marry Miss Bingley. Mrs. Bennet will practically live with you, and neither of you will have the heart to ask her to leave."

"You exaggerate. In any case, I do not care if Mrs. Bennet comes to live with us, if it means that I have Jane. Darcy, you cannot imagine the torment I am enduring. *You* have never been in love. *You* have never cared enough for any woman to want to sacrifice the world for her."

Darcy began to pace the room, full of agitation. He wanted to laugh with the irony of it all. If Bingley only knew the torments he had endured over Elizabeth Bennet! He was sure no one at all – certainly not Bingley, whose emotions were closer to the surface – could even understand the depth of his despair at Miss Bennet's refusal. Only the conviction that it was the best possible thing she could have done to deflect him from a moment of insanity kept him going. Her cruelty only served to remind him of the very reason he should not have given in to his emotions.

"The day will come when you will thank me for saving you from social disaster, Charles. I know you cannot see clearly now because of the pain, but there will be a day when you will be very glad that I kept you from Miss Bennet."

"Damn you, Darcy. I wish you would get off your high horse and be human for once. One cannot go through life thinking only of social status. Where would all the nobler emotions be – the emotions that have been the inspiration for poetry and the best of human attainment throughout history? If it were up to you, not a word of poetry would every have been written from the beginning of time. I tell you, Darcy, I will not hear a word more from someone who has as much sensitivity as a bit of rock. Leave me alone. Go preach your hollow view of the world somewhere else."

The injustice of this drove him beyond endurance. Darcy felt the sting of it like salt in a wound.

He could stay silent no longer.

"You are not the only person in the world smitten by love, Charles. Long before you even knew you felt any regard for Miss Bennet, I had tumbled headlong into love." Bingley, startled, turned and sat up in bed. "Yes. You believe me indifferent, but you know nothing. You claim to be a friend, yet you have never guessed. I have been kinder to you than to myself."

Darcy knew he should say nothing more, but he could not help himself any more than a waterfall can prevent itself from hurtling off the side of a mountain.

"You may well look surprised, but I have endured far more than you. And at whose hands? At the hands of none other than Miss Elizabeth Bennet!" He turned away from Charles' astonishment. "Remember, it was you who introduced me to her, who encouraged me to dance with her, if you will recall. And to what end? Only to have me humiliated and humbled by that love."

As Charles began to say something, Darcy held up his hand.

"You do not know the half of it, Charles. There is worse to come. Not only was I foolish enough to fall in love with her. I was foolish enough to believe that my suit was welcome – that she would be delighted if I were to offer her my hand in marriage. Little did I know that she despised me so much she could not wait to be rid of me." Darcy swallowed hard. His hands were trembling and the lump that rose up in his throat was full of tears desperate to be shed.

He turned and left the room, slamming the door behind him. He would not embarrass himself and actually have Bingley see him cry.

Outside in the long passageway, he leaned his forehead against the cool paint of the wall, struggling to restrain the sobs rising up inside him. He would not cry. He had not cried for years, not since his mother had died and he had realized for the first time that he would never see her again. Men did not cry. At least, *he* did not.

He brought up the side of his fists and struck the soft pads at the unyielding wall. Pain resonated through him. His body sagged against the wall. He was so tired. Tired of fighting. Tired of trying to pretend nothing was wrong. Tired of holding his shattered soul curled up into a tight ball inside him.

The door opened.

"Darcy?" said Bingley.

Darcy stood up straight with an overwhelming effort. The muscles of his throat hurt so badly from forcing the tears back down that he could not make a sound.

"Darcy, I'm sorry. I didn't realize. You should have told me."

Bingley was standing there so distressingly vulnerable he could have been the same little boy that Darcy had first taken under his wing at school, looking lost and completely out of place amongst the aristocrats who were born and bred to centuries of privilege and wealth.

Darcy shook his head.

"I wanted to protect you," he whispered. "I did not want you to come to harm. You're like a brother to me."

Then, unable to trust himself any further, he turned on his heel and walked away.

Chapter Eleven

Either Caroline had powers of divination or she had been listening for his footsteps, for no sooner had he reached the bottom of the stairs when she appeared out of thin air, as if by magic.

She was the last person he wanted to deal with at the moment, but he could not be uncivil to her either, not in her own home and not without good reason.

"Mr. Darcy," said Caroline. "You look displeased. Has Charles been disagreeable? You must not take it to heart. If there is anyone who can bring him out of the doldrums it is you. He admires you greatly."

"I'm aware of that, Caroline. However, I have just remembered an urgent appointment."

To his relief, he was enough master of himself for his words to come out clearly, with only a hint of hoarseness to give him away.

"But what about—. I thought you had something to say to me? Are you leaving so soon? Mr. Darcy?"

"Later," said Darcy, taking his hat and walking stick from Evans and making swift use of the door that opened before him.

"But I poured you some tea," said Caroline behind him. "Exactly the way you like it."

Tea? That was not what he needed. No, what he needed were a few bottles of gin to drown his sorrows. Not that he had ever had a drop of the blue ruin before, but he knew enough young gentlemen who thought it the height of fashion to visit the gin shops. Perhaps this was the right time to discover the secret of its appeal – to lose himself in a public alehouse where no one knew him or cared.

Fortunately, he had not been reduced to such dire straits as all that. Not yet. Besides, he could hardly let himself fall to pieces when he had only just roused Bingley from a similar state. St. James' and his club would be a far better option. A brisk walk first would provide the opportunity to find self-control. He would have to employ an iron will if he did not wish to make an exhibition of himself at his club.

He had walked round Berkeley Square several times before he realized he was quite literally walking in circles. By then some of his turmoil had quieted down, enough for him to realize that he had left poor Georgiana behind without a word. How could he have forgotten her so completely? He knew she already thought his behavior rather odd. This incident confirmed it. It would be considerably worse if she and Miss Bingley had happened to look out of the window and discovered him walking around the square like a bedlamite.

As if to confirm his worries, the door to the Bingley townhouse opened before him and Bingley emerged, fully dressed and looking amused.

"I saw you from the window, staggering around like a hound chasing its own tail, and thought you might be in need of rescue," said Bingley.

"Ah," said Darcy. "I see I have been noticed. Will the ladies be joining us?"

No doubt they had been enjoying the spectacle from the window as well.

"No, they will not. They are in the piano room singing a duet, completely unaware they have missed the opportunity of a lifetime to see you make a cake of yourself."

"Thank heavens for small mercies," said Darcy, letting out a sigh.

He was spared that much, at least. And he supposed his visit had done some good if it had dragged Charles out of bed. Even if Charles looked rather the worse for wear.

His gaze alighted on Charles' cravat. A strong sense of the ridiculousness of both their situations struck him and he began to laugh.

"You have quite a tangle there. It looks like a blind man tied it with one hand while doing a jig."

Charles looked down at the indistinct knot, frowning, then burst into laughter.

"You're not far wrong, Darcy. I was tying it while looking out of the window."

"I hope you do not expect me to appear in public with you like that, Charles," said Darcy.

"You cannot let me down now, Darcy, not when you promised me some amusement."

"I will wait for you at the end of the road while your valet attempts to repair the damage, as long as you promise not to alert the ladies to my presence."

"Very well," said Charles. "Where shall we go?"

Darcy had no idea at all for entertainment – he had not even glanced at the cards on the mantle to see if he was invited anywhere, if there was anyone still left in Town to invite him. It was too early for invitations, in any case. Hyde Park at the fashionable hour should contain a few

"If you're so eager for entertainment, Charles, you name it and I'm at your disposal. What will it be? Women? Cards? Vauxhall? A masquerade ball? Fencing? Personally an hour of pugilism with Gentleman Jack on Bond Street might be just the thing I need."

"Later, perhaps? To be honest, Darcy, I don't wish to go anywhere particular. I only want to sit outdoors in the shade of a tree and talk. I have been shut in my room alone. I thought no one understood what I was going through, but now here you are, experiencing the same thing!" Bingley grinned. "I say, how very fortunate. We can compare experiences. I want to find out exactly what happened with Miss Elizabeth."

Darcy did not want to compare anything. He was relieved to have admitted his feelings at last to Bingley, but he did not have any further need to pour out his emotions as Bingley seemed to expect.

"I do not think it a good idea to go back to your house – your sister will be bound to ask me a hundred questions and will not leave us in peace."

He envisioned Caroline chasing after him with a cup of tea.

"I said I wanted to be outdoors, did I not? We shall sit in the square. No one will venture there at this time of the day. Except, perhaps, for Lady Jersey, who may have witnessed your odd meanderings from the window of her house at number 38 and is overcome with curiosity. Lord, that woman loves to discover the latest gossip."

"I am quite capable of dealing with Lady Jersey," said Darcy. "However, I cannot say the same about the garden." He eyed the private square and the spiked iron railings that guarded it. "I would rather not be impaled climbing in, and you cannot return home for the key without arousing curiosity."

Charles reached for a key which was protruding out of his waist pocket.

"You do not have to fear impalement," said Charles, with a flourish of his arm. "I brought the key with me just in case."

Darcy's hand went automatically to his own waist pocket as he felt for the folded paper folded there. He remembered his original purpose in coming to London. He did have something to talk about after all. He would discuss his matrimonial plans with Bingley and the two of them would compile lists of the qualities of their future brides together.

As they walked towards a bench, Darcy explained what it was he was thinking of.

"Surely not, Darcy? You want me to write down a list of the qualities I would wish for in a bride? Of all the ill-conceived ideas in the world! How could I do so when all I can think of is my angel?"

He sat down on a bench next to Darcy then jumped up again full of agitation.

"Absolutely not," Bingley continued. "I can understand why you would wish to give up all thoughts of love after your experience, but you must not assume that I am in the same situation." He took a few steps forward, returned to cast a wild glance at Darcy, walked away, and idly began kicking one of the legs another bench. Finally he came and stood in front of Darcy. "I do believe I have come to a decision. You will not like it, and neither will my sisters, but for once I will go my own way. I cannot simply give up Miss Bennet without at least being certain that she does not care for me. I know you have told me that is the case, and I trust your judgment in most matters, but this is something I must discover for myself."

"But Charles, even if she did care for you, that would not change the fact that she is completely inappropriate for you if you mean to advance socially. You know firsthand what it is like to be treated as an outsider by others. You remember what it was like in school."

"In school, I had good friends like you. That is all I could have wished for. Besides, I do not see how Miss Bennet will interfere with my social ambitions. She is a perfectly well-mannered young lady and she is the daughter of a gentleman, which is more than can be said for my father. The Bennets may not be appropriate for a Darcy, but they are quite good enough for the Bingleys."

"Your sisters would disagree, particularly Caroline. You have to admit it – Caroline's marriage prospects will be damaged by a marriage like this. If you do not mind having Mrs. Bennet living in your pocket, you must at least wait until your sister is married so that it does not affect her prospects as well. She is in a very delicate social situation and stands to lose the most."

Charles considered this.

"Very well. I will wait. But it tries my patience. How do I know Miss Bennet will not marry in the meanwhile?"

"It will do you good, Bingley, to learn some patience. If you truly love Miss Bennet, then this will be the best possible test of your affections."

Bingley looked so unhappy that Darcy relented.

"Very well. We will just have to find a way to communicate with her. I promise I will think of something. Then you will know at least if she is willing to wait for you."

He had the idea he was going to regret his promise.

~~X~~

"Oh, look. How very droll," said Miss Bingley. "Your brother and mine are sitting in the garden. Whatever are they doing there? I did not know Charles was with Mr. Darcy. They have been very mysterious about their comings and goings, have they not? I have half a mind to join them, to discover what they are up to. No, of course we shall not. Though I would very much like to know what Mr. Darcy could be saying to my brother that he could not say in the house. What do you suppose it can be?"

Georgiana knew what conjectures Caroline was making. She had to put a stop to it.

"I know my brother and Mr. Bingley have quarreled. It was the reason my brother decided to come to London. I am very happy that they appear to be mending the breach."

"Dear Georgiana, you cannot believe that your brother came all the way to London merely because of a quarrel! There is more to the matter, depend upon it. They would not be so deep in conversation simply because of a quarrel. Gentlemen are not like us ladies. They have no need for conversation or gossip. They sort out their quarrels in other ways, like fencing or racing."

It is a remarkable fact of the human mind that it can always find a way to justify what it believes. Georgiana could not fault Caroline's statement. There was enough truth in it to make it impossible for her to argue, but she knew that Caroline was deluding herself.

She thought it best not to respond.

"Now, I really must know what our two gentlemen wish to do," said Caroline, going to the window and looking out from behind the curtain. "Should I tell Cook to expect the two of you for dinner or will you be going home?"

Since Darcy seemed to have forgotten her existence for the moment, Georgiana did not know what he planned. In fact, she was quite vexed with him for leaving her alone with Caroline on the very first day of their arrival in London. She had hoped they would be having more time together.

"I think it likely that we will be dining with you," she said.

Caroline looked very pleased at the news. She hurried away to give instructions to the cook.

The front door opened and her brother could be heard along with Bingley. Darcy was laughing loudly as if he did not have a care in the world, with no evidence of the dark mood that had been hovering over him like a cloud.

A suspicion crossed Georgiana's mind. She had been dismissive about Caroline's assumptions, but what if she was entirely wrong?

What if William meant to ask Caroline Bingley to marry him?

Chapter Twelve

Two days later, determined to do what he could to fulfil his agreement with Bingley, Darcy called at the Bingley's townhouse again. Bingley was out, but both Caroline and Mrs. Hurst, he was informed, were there.

He found Miss Bingley alone in the morning room, occupied in doing a charcoal sketch of Berkeley Square. This would be a good opportunity to ask her for her advice about choosing the right wife, but for some reason he seemed unable to bring himself to do it.

Having complimented her on the accuracy of her sketch and asked a few polite questions, Darcy came quickly to the purpose of his visit.

"Miss Bingley, do you happen to have the direction of Miss Bennet's relatives? The ones you called on? Their name has slipped my mind."

"You mean the tradespeople? I do not think so," said Miss Bingley, in a haughty voice. "Since we no longer required it, I discarded Miss Bennet's note. Though I cannot imagine why you would wish to know it."

"I would prefer not to have your brother sink into melancholy. I would like to find out if Miss Bennet is still in residence."

He thought he saw relief on her face. In any case, some of the arrogance disappeared.

"I wish I could help you, Mr. Darcy. I no longer have the address."

"Surely you must remember the street name and general direction."

"Unfortunately, it has slipped my mind."

"What slipped your mind, Caroline?" said Mrs. Hurst, coming into the room rather suddenly, presumably to act as chaperone to her sister.

"Mr. Darcy requires the address of Miss Bennet's relations." Darcy noticed her gesturing to her sister. Was she trying to warn her sister not to reveal the location?

Whatever the case may have been, Mrs. Hurst chose not to heed the warning.

"Oh, I remember it perfectly well. Why, we were recalling it the other day when we debated whether to call on Miss Bennet again. I will write it down for you, Mr. Darcy."

Caroline turned away with a peevish expression. Darcy could only conclude she wanted to discontinue all connection to the Bennets.

It did not matter if she did. For now, the main thing was that he had the address.

"I am very grateful to you, Mrs. Hurst."

Caroline, as if realizing that her behavior hardly recommended her to the object of her attentions, suddenly turned and smiled at Darcy.

"Why, yes, now that you mention it, Louisa, I do recall how to go there. I would be happy to accompany you, Mr. Darcy, if you intend to call on the Gardiners."

The last person he wished to accompany him was Caroline. "Thank you, Miss Bingley, but there is no need. This is not a social call. I merely intend to enquire if Jane Bennet is still in London."

Miss Bingley was not pleased. However, she consoled herself by inviting him for dinner, an invitation Darcy readily accepted since he had already agreed to dine with Bingley at home.

Though a huge part of him hoped that somehow, miraculously, Elizabeth Bennet would be at her uncle's house and that he would be invited to dine with the Gardiners instead.

The Gardiners resided on Gracechurch Street, in Cheapside. It was not the most fashionable part of London, certainly, but it was one of the most opulent and wealthy areas; it was where the fashionable went to shop. Darcy himself had been there often enough on shopping expeditions for china and furnishings.

Darcy chose to descend from the carriage on the street corner. He preferred to walk the rest of the way. It would give his skittish nerves a chance to settle before he located the address.

By and by Darcy found himself in front of an elegant white stucco townhouse with shrubs and herbaceous borders and a dark blue door. Everything about it spoke of gentility and refined wealth. There was no vulgar ornamentation, no exaggeration of the simple classical lines of the façade. One could not fault the Gardiners' taste. There was no sign of the shop about it.

He started to climb up the small flight of steps leading to the door then stopped. What if Elizabeth was there? All these months in which he had worked hard to achieve some kind of calm would be cast away if he set eyes on her.

Far better to have Bingley call on the Gardiners.

He turned on his tale and walked down the street, turned onto Cheapside and continued until he found himself in front of the domed cathedral of St. Paul's. Without thinking of it, he entered and sat at one of the pews, hoping to find a measure of peace that would help him decide, but the black and white checkered pattern of the floor and the multiple arches to both sides of him seemed to mock him. The floor was like a giant chess game – full of unpredictable moves with unanticipated consequences. Each arch seemed to represent a different possibility, a different doorway he could take, none of them conclusive.

In the end he was left to his own devices. There was no sudden illumination that ruled decisively on one plan of action over the other. He rose from the pew and walked slowly down the long nave, his footsteps echoing in the quiet.

"Can I help you, my son?" said a man in the scarlet chimere of a bishop as he passed him. "Do you need spiritual guidance?"

Darcy shook his head. "Thank you, sir," he said. "I must make a decision, and no one can help me with that."

Something of his desperate uncertainty must have appeared on his face because the bishop gave him a sympathetic glance.

106

"Sometimes we must choose the more difficult path," said the bishop.

Which was the more difficult path? Following one's heart or following the dictates of society? He could not even answer that question, let alone make the decision.

When he walked out through the open doorway he found it was raining. The streets had turned grimy and for a moment as he emerged the clacking of pattens against the cobbles sounded like the clapping of many hands.

He returned to Gracechurch Street and to the stucco house with the blue door and walked up the steps. He realized now what he had not noticed before, that there was no knocker – an indication that the family was not in residence. That did not mean, however, that there was no one there. The Bennet nieces might be there with a chaperon, though part of him knew it was very unlikely.

Darcy tugged at the doorbell, his heart clattering like horses' hooves. If Elizabeth was there—.

The bell echoed through the house. From somewhere inside, slow footsteps slowly came closer.

A butler in dignified dark green and gold livery opened the door.

"May I help you, sir?"

It was soon apparent that neither he nor Bingley were to be satisfied. Darcy's enquiries came to nothing. The family was away from home – they were travelling in the North and would not be back for several weeks. None of the Bennets were in residence. The butler could not provide Darcy with an address for where the Gardiners were residing in the North since they were on the road without a fixed residence.

Darcy turned away with a sense of bitter disappointment. It was only now that his hopes had been dashed that he realized how much stock he had placed in seeing Elizabeth Bennet. It was entirely irrational, of course. Why would she happen to be in London just because he wished it so?

He had to remind himself that his actual purpose in visiting the Gardiners had not been to see Elizabeth but to help Bingley with the object of his interest.

There was nothing to be done. Bingley could not correspond with Miss Bennet directly. Darcy had hoped to convinced Mr. or Mrs. Gardiner to convey a message, but that, it appeared was impossible.

If Bingley wished to convey a message, he would have to meet a member of Miss Bennet's family, and Darcy had not heard of other relations in London.

Confound these social rules! It would have been the simplest thing in the world to send Miss Bennet a letter, but of course society liked to complicate matters. A letter between a single young man and a single lady was improper.

There was nothing more to be done here. Perhaps, after all, it would in fact be in their best interest to go to Netherfield.

His treacherous heart sang with joy at the thought of meeting Elizabeth Bennet again.

~~X~~

Georgiana had imagined that, with the scarcity of fashionable people in London, and her limited circle of friends, she would not be likely to run into anyone she knew. Thus when she went with Mrs. Annesley to Finsbury Square to acquire some new printed music and some books, she was surprised to be hailed from a passing carriage that had now stopped.

"Miss Darcy!"

There was no mistaking that nasal voice. Georgiana's immediate instinct was to pretend deafness. Next to her, Mrs. Annesley pretended deafness as well.

"Miss Darcy! Mrs. Annesley!"

Georgiana heard the door of the carriage open.

"Hurry," she said to Mrs. Annesley. "If we go into Lackington Allen, we can hide behind the maps."

As fate would have it, a sudden downpour rescued them. As they entered the giant bookshop, Georgiana cast a quick glance through the window and saw Miss Marshall scurrying back to the waiting carriage.

"How very fortunate," she said, with a grin. She knew proper young ladies did not grin, but she could not help it.

"I am afraid you will not be able to escape her acquaintance, however, now that she knows you are in London."

Georgiana sighed. "I know, but at least she will not ruin my visit to the Temple of Muses by giving me advice on what books to read and what music to select." She looked around her with a sense of excitement. "You know, Mrs. Annesley, this is my favorite place in London."

Mrs. Annesley laughed. "I am well aware of that. I have been dragged here too many times to mention."

"You need not pretend you dislike it, for I know you do not. It is usually I who am compelled to drag you away when it is time to leave."

Mrs. Annesley put her hand on her charge's arm, smiling. "You cannot imagine how pleased I am to see you are laughing these days. You passed through so many months of unhappiness I despaired of you ever recovering."

Georgiana nodded, turning abruptly serious. "Wickham did not deserve a single moment of my thoughts, let alone my unhappiness, but I could not help it. I imagine he did not feel anything at all, except anger at the prospect of being deprived of a vast sum of money."

"Well, it is all behind us now," remarked her companion.

"Which is precisely why I do not wish to spend a moment in this wonderful place being unhappy." She looked around the vast room in anticipation. "Come on, Mrs. Annesley. What are you waiting for?"

When they arrived home two hours later, carrying precious string-tied parcels, the housekeeper, Mrs. Lennox, met them in the doorway.

"You have visitors waiting for you, Miss Darcy. They insisted on coming in. Said they knew you well from Pemberley."

"From Pemberley? Who could they be?"

She groaned. The answer was obvious. "It must be Lady Renwick and Miss Marshall."

It was not Lady Renwick, however. Miss Marshall and another lady awaited them in the parlor. The stranger was wandering around the room, picking up objects and examining them closely. Georgiana could not help feeling that this person was evaluating each piece to see how much Fitzwilliam Darcy was worth.

"Miss Darcy," said the mother, with a nasal twang, tripping across the room with outstretched arms. "I have heard so much about you! I am delighted to finally meet you. Dear Elinor won't stop talking about you."

Georgiana had to make a supreme effort not to step back as the tall lady came bearing down on her. She could see a distinct resemblance between mother and daughter – they were both like quacking geese, with long necks and nasal speech.

"I hope you do not mind us calling on you so unceremoniously, Miss Darcy. May I call you Georgiana? After all, you are just like my daughter. We do not consider ourselves strangers, do we, Elinor? I feel quite as if I have always known you."

"I have been at Pemberley so often," said Miss Marshall with a small titter, "the inhabitants of Lambton may well believe I live there."

Live there? At Pemberley? When she had visited their house no more than three or four times?

"I would almost envy Elinor her ease in making new friends," said her mother fondly. "Except that I am also blessed with the same ability." She gave a little laugh. "Is she not the most sociable of creatures, Georgiana?"

Georgian seethed at the intimacy implied by Mrs. Marshall's use of her name. However, years of training came to the fore and prevented her from being uncivil.

"Miss Marshall makes herself at home wherever she goes," she said.

Mrs. Marshall beamed as if Georgiana had praised her daughter highly.

"You know she already has several eligible young men showing interest in her, and the season has not yet begun. Of course, she will have nothing to do with them. She has her sights set out higher. If your brother does manage to gain her attention, he should consider himself fortunate.

Elinor will have to have her season, of course – I would never wish to deprive her of the balls and the musical soirees and all the wonderful things every debutante dreams of. No matter how much she may desire it, I will not allow her to be formally engaged before the season has ended."

Georgiana was shocked at Mrs. Marshall's audacity. Clearly Miss Marshall was under the distinct impression that Darcy had intended to offer for her. The worst of it was that she might be right. She knew Darcy was still considering her as the future mistress of Pemberley and, despite all his denials, it was quite possible that Miss Marshall was the reason for their precipitous journey to town.

Or it could be Caroline he intended to marry. Georgiana could not discount that possibility either.

At this point, she would welcome Caroline into the family with open arms. Perhaps she needed to provide some assistance to Miss Bingley, after all.

~~x~~

Darcy entered the house full of renewed energy. A trip to Netherfield would solve Mr. Bingley's problem, and for him – well a glimpse of Elizabeth would cure him once and for all of his obsession. Was there not a saying: "Absence makes the heart grow fonder?" His obsession with Elizabeth was exaggerated by her absence. In her absence, he had endowed her with all kind of qualities that would not live up to the reality of seeing her. If he were to see her, he would be cured.

"Is Miss Darcy in?"

"Yes, she is," said Franklin. "But she—."

Darcy waved the butler away, too impatient to hear whatever it was he had to say. He needed to inform Georgiana of his latest plans at once. Now that he had broken his silence with Bingley, perhaps it was time to tell Georgiana the truth about Elizabeth as well.

111

Darcy strode into the salon. He was expecting to see Georgiana alone with Mrs. Annesley, but as the door opened, he checked his stride, taken completely by surprise.

"Oh, Mr. Darcy. It is very fortunate that you came just now. We were on the verge of leaving," said Miss Marshall. "Allow me to introduce my mother."

Miss Marshall's mother was an older version of her daughter, with thin haughty brows and a very long neck. She was a rather handsome lady with a great deal of energy.

Darcy bowed and considered the ways of Fortune. He had been on the verge of committing the utmost folly by following Miss Bennet to Meryton. Instead, he had been given an opportune reminder of the resolution he had made, which was to marry sensibly and not to allow emotion to dictate his future.

"I am delighted to meet you," he said, meaning every word as he considered how close to the abyss he had ventured.

"We came to call on Georgiana to welcome her to London, and to issue an invitation to you both for dinner tomorrow. It will be a small party – nothing formal, of course, since my daughter is not yet out. Elinor kindly suggested that, since Georgiana is locked away in the country most of the time, she may be in desperate need of amusement. A dinner party like this would be just the thing for her."

"We would be delighted to accept," said Darcy. "Wouldn't we, Georgiana?"

Georgiana had her stubborn look. He had the feeling she was going to say no. The Marshalls were charming, considerate people. Georgiana should be glad of this opportunity to meet people in a small, discreet setting.

"Delighted," said Georgiana, with a polite smile.

"Have you had refreshments brought up?" he asked.

"Yes, thank you, Mr. Darcy. Your sister has been most obliging. Such a pretty thing, and so tall, which is always an advantage because you can be noticed in a crowded room. When you are having clothes prepared, Georgiana, you must make sure to add plenty of frills to

112

counteract the appearance of tallness." She leaned over and patted Georgiana on the arm. "Poor dear, and to think you have no mother to advise you. It must all be very bewildering. But you need not be afraid, and I will take you under my wing. I do feel sorry for you."

Georgiana had too big blotches of red on her cheeks. Darcy was all too familiar with those blotches. They appeared most frequently when Aunt Catherine was around, though of course Mrs. Marshall was not at all like their aunt.

"As long as she does not purloin my admirers," said Miss Marshall, with a nervous titter.

"There will be more than enough young men worshiping at the altar of both young ladies, I am certain," said Darcy, with the utmost civility.

"Good," said Mrs. Marshall, "I look forward to seeing you tomorrow, then."

"I am very sorry, Mrs. Marshall. This is embarrassing, but I have just recalled a prior engagement of ours. We will have to decline your kind invitation, Mrs. Marshall," said Georgiana. "We have already promised to attend the theatre with friends. Kemble is playing *Julius Caesar*, and I am particularly eager to see him in that role. Remember, William, that you agreed to accompany us?"

"Yes," said Darcy, completely taken aback by this sudden volte-face on the part of his little sister, but not wishing to contradict her in public, "I am afraid my sister is quite correct. The engagement *had* slipped my mind. Unfortunately, my hands are tied, but I hope to have the pleasure of dining with you another night."

"Well," said Mrs. Marshall. "What a disappointment, to be sure." She rose abruptly to her feet and Miss Marshall followed. "Naturally, there is no hurry. I will send round an invitation for early next week. I hope you do not have any prior engagements?"

"We would be delighted to join you," said Darcy, firmly.

Mrs. Marshall gave Georgiana a triumphant smile.

Curtseying elegantly, the two ladies sailed from the room.

Darcy waited until the front door closed then turned to his sister.

"What is the matter with you, Georgiana? What nonsense was that about a friend and going to the theater? And implicating me, too! Is this because you are shy and disinclined to meet new people? You must start somewhere, and you certainly cannot prevent me from accepting an invitation after I have already agreed to it."

The two red blotches on her cheeks intensified.

"It has nothing to do with being disinclined to meet new people. It so happens that I *do* have an engagement to attend the theatre with Caroline Bingley. However, even if I did not, I do not care for Mrs. Marshall at all and I care even less for Miss Marshall. If you wish to marry her, that is your affair, but I would rather spend my time in London in another manner."

Darcy was at a loss to understand his sister's intense dislike for Miss Marshall. Georgiana rarely took a dislike to anyone.

"I'll be the first to admit that Miss Marshall is rather opinionated, but I consider that an advantage for a lady of her position in society," said Darcy. "Our mother's side of the family has always had strong women. Look at Aunt Catherine. You never met our grandmother. She, too, was a woman with very determined opinions. I remember her well. I prefer a woman who knows her own mind to a simpering Miss."

With a vague feeling of guilt, he felt for the folded paper in his waistcoat pocket. He had scratched out that quality on his list.

"So do I," said Georgiana, "but I do not like it when people – ladies or gentlemen – are so decided in their opinions that they do not respect the opinions of others."

"You have taken a considerable dislike to Miss Marshall, but what will you do if I do decide to take her as my bride?"

"If I have no choice in the matter, I will deal with it as best as I can, but until then I can only hope you will see sense and realize that Miss Marshall is not the right person for you. I do not believe she will make you happy."

Nothing would ever make him happy again. He had accepted that. Life was not about happiness. It was about duty. His choice must reflect that. His duty was towards Pemberley above all else. His own happiness was irrelevant.

Georgiana was looking at him with such an earnest expression on her little face he could not quarrel with her. He reached out and touched her cheek with the back of his hand.

"Once upon a time I, too, thought happiness was possible," said Darcy, feeling the pain of his words echo through his very soul, "but I have learned that the pursuit of happiness is nothing but a dream. We must cherish what we have, but each of us has a role to play in the world and we must play it the best way we can. Sometimes that means we must sacrifice our own desires or wishes for something bigger than ourselves. In my case, it is Pemberley. In choosing a wife I am choosing a mistress for Pemberley. That is why I cannot choose with my heart." He stopped and lifted Georgiana's chin up so that her eyes were forced to meet his. "We do not always love wisely, little sister, as well you know."

He knew from the expression in her eyes that she was thinking of Wickham. For a moment, she looked unhappy, then that sharp tilted of her chin returned.

"We cannot always choose whom we love," she replied, "but if we are lucky enough to have any choice in whom we marry, then it is our duty to make our selection wisely and not allow bitterness to cloud our judgment."

With this, his little Sister rose and flounced out of the room, leaving him to ponder in bewilderment what he had done wrong.

Chapter Thirteen

The sky was overcast. Even though he was inside the carriage, Darcy did not particularly wish to be caught in the rain. After these heavy summer downpours, the roads could turn into a morass of mud within minutes and he hoped to be in Pemberley before the rain slowed him down.

He had received an express from Mr. Arnold, his Steward, calling him back to Pemberley. This was the busiest time of the year on the land and there were several urgent decisions awaiting his approval.

Fortunately, his brief trip to town had been fruitful. He had repaired his rift with Bingley, he had met Miss Marshall's mother, and he had averted the temptation of going to Netherfield. Moreover, he had put together a group, including the Bingleys, who would be joining him at Pemberley in a matter of days. Georgiana seemed to have attached herself to Caroline, to the extent of preferring to travel up in the Bingley's carriage rather than coming with him. Not bad for a few days' work.

He was turning a new leaf. He could feel it in his blood.

The sound of commotion ahead reached him. The carriage slowed and came to an abrupt halt, just in time to avoid a collision with a hay cart which had tipped over and scattered bales all over the road. They were more fortunate than the carriage ahead of them had been. It lay on its side in a ditch.

An accident with a hay cart. It was not uncommon during the hay-making season. Hay carts were often overloaded, and it was not unusual for the hay to topple down onto the road.

Darcy leapt out of the carriage. Whoever those unfortunate people were, he had to help them immediately. A man sat by the side of the road, looking desperate.

When he saw Darcy, he came to his feet, looking dazed.

Darcy recognized him immediately as Mr. Coulter, a small farmer. From the expression on Mr. Coulter's face, he had to assume the worst – that whoever was travelling in the carriage had met an unpleasant end.

"What happened?"

"He's dead, sir. He just collapsed, sir, suddenly. A moment ago, he war battin' along, and now he's dead."

"Are you entirely certain?"

"As certain as anything, sir. I should know my own horse. He won't be getting up na more."

Now that he knew to look for it, Darcy could make out the shape of a horse, lying on its side in the road, half-covered with straw.

"I see. I'm sorry about your loss, Mr. Coulter, but what about the coachman and the occupants of the carriage?"

"I don't know. I didn't think to look, sir, not with what happened to poor Thunder."

Darcy bit back a disparaging remark. For Mr. Coulter, the loss of a horse might mean a serious loss of income especially now the harvest was beginning. Darcy could not entirely blame him for his neglect. There was not a moment to lose, however. Their assistance might be the difference between life and death.

"My men and I will handle the overturned carriage. Mr. Coulter, your assistance is needed with the team. You need to hold the horses so they don't bolt."

Darcy looked around for the coachman of the other carriage. There was no sign of him. Poor man, he had probably been crushed under the carriage as it overturned.

Just then there were muffled thumps from the carriage. Darcy ran towards it. The door, which was now on the top of the carriage, was slowly pushed open and a lady's head appeared. She appeared to be in her late thirties, with fine delicate features and an elegant manner.

Thank heavens she had come to no serious harm.

Darcy reached out to her quickly.

"If you will give me your hand, madam, I will help you climb out."

When she turned to face him, however, he saw there was blood on her head, and a large purple bruise covered the left side of her face.

He concealed his alarm at the sight and focused his attention on assisting her.

At this angle it was very difficult to keep the door open while she struggled to lever herself out, even with both him and Ebenezer helping. Finally, somehow, they managed.

No sooner had she scrambled out when she gestured towards the inside, her face drawn with worry.

"My husband is still inside. He has been injured. And my niece. He fell on top of her. I fear—"

"We will do everything we can to assist them. Can you walk unaided?"

"Yes. I don't require anything. But I want to help the others."

"You will only be in the way," said Darcy, gently. "Better for you to sit down. You have clearly suffered a blow to the head. We do not know what repercussions it may have."

"Very well," said the woman. She straightened out her clothes and proceeded to sit down on a bale of hay. Darcy could not help admiring her restraint and the dignified nature of her response to a very distressing situation.

It was now the turn of the husband to be rescued.

"Careful, now," he said to young Ebenezer. "We don't want to dislodge the carriage and cause further injury."

With him blocking the only current source of light, it was dark inside and Darcy could only just make out the form of the woman's husband. He had been knocked out and was lying sprawled against the bottom window, a dead weight. There was a woman's arm extended out from under him.

"It doesn't look good for the woman, sir," remarked Ebenezer. "Not with that weight crushing her against the glass. Especially if the glass is broken."

He spoke quietly. Darcy nodded grimly. "It doesn't, but we can't let them know that. The sooner we get the husband out, the faster we can deal with the niece."

Ebenezer, who was the smaller of the two, slid carefully into the carriage, making sure not to upset the precarious balance as it teetered over the edge. Ebenezer felt the man's pulse.

"He's alive, sir."

"Good," said Darcy. "Let's get him out."

Ebenezer struggled to lift up the man, but only succeeded in propping him up against the seat.

"He's a dead weight. I can't lift him alone. I think you're going to have to come in, sir. It will be very awkward, but I can't see another way."

As Darcy started to climb in, the carriage shifted. Darcy held his breath and froze in place, praying that the shift was not enough to cause a downslide. He tried not to panic as he imagined the carriage careening down the hillside. The moment stretched onwards, an eternity of waiting. Just as he began to feel it was safe enough for him to move, the carriage shifted again.

Darcy closed his eyes and stayed completely still.

The moment stretched on. Nothing. The carriage did not shift again.

"I am not certain I can move any further. It is too much of a risk. If you will find a way to shift him so I can grab hold of his arms then we can contrive to get him out between us."

It took some time, but somehow they managed to do the impossible. It worried Darcy that they might be injuring him further by moving him about in this manner, but there was no other alternative. They could not leave him. If it started to rain – as it was threatening to do, since the sky was overcast – the embankment might turn muddy and the carriage might well slide down.

As they lifted the man to safety, Darcy heard the niece stirring.

"Better not move," he instructed her. "We'll be back as soon as we have helped your uncle."

"Is he—?" asked the wife, clearly bracing herself for bad news.

119

"He's alive. The pulse seems strong enough," said Darcy.

"Thank heavens," she said, grasping her husband's hand and walking along with them.

As they laid the unconscious man in Darcy's carriage, she looked up and gave a small cry.

"Lizzy! You're alright!"

Darcy put down the man he was carrying on the carriage seat with a thump and turned round. Confound it! He had told the niece to stay put. If the carriage toppled backwards, she could be killed.

The head of a young woman was protruding from the top.

His heart stopped beating. It paused for so long he thought he would die. It resumed. And stopped. Then it began to pound so hard he was certain everyone around him could hear it.

It could not be.

Yet there was no mistaking those chestnut brown locks. He stood frozen in place as Elizabeth Bennet reached out with her arms and tried to pull herself out of the carriage. She was looking at her aunt. She had not yet seen him.

"How is my uncle?" she asked.

"He is alive," said her aunt.

A joyful look lit up her face.

Darcy did not want her to see him. He did not want the joy to be replaced by contempt. He remembered all too well her expression when he had last seen her and he never wanted to see it again.

He held his breath.

Never mind about the contempt. He wanted her desperately to look at him, to see him, to know he still existed in the world. He would endure the pain, he would endure anything right now, just to be the object of her gaze again.

Elizabeth.

"I could do with some assistance," she said, tartly, not looking at him at all. She was occupied with finding a foothold to climb out.

She slid back down with a cry of pain.

He knew he should assist her but he could not move. His legs were like lead. Until she saw him, he could not move.

Elizabeth's head reappeared.

"Are you going to help me, aunt?"

Her aunt must have gestured towards him, because suddenly Elizabeth's expression sharpened and shifted.

A pair of fine dark eyes met his.

Everything around him shifted and disappeared. He was trapped by her gaze. He trembled as his whole being waited for her to decide what to do with him.

"Mr. Darcy," she said, turning towards him,

There was blood on the other side of her face. Terror for her replaced everything else and without knowing how he did it he was at her side in an instant.

He could not bear it. If she was hurt in any way—.

"Do not move. Do nothing. Allow us to lift you out," he said, urgently. Where was Ebenezer when he needed him?

"I am not incapacitated," she said, laughing shakily.

"Mr. Darcy?" Ebenezer had come running at once. Good lad.

Darcy slid down into the carriage next to her and held her up by the waist as Ebenezer pulled her out. He was exquisitely aware of her as his hand brushed against her side. His whole body vibrated to her closeness. His muscles ached with the effort of holding back, of doing only what was appropriate. He had dreamt so many times of holding her. It was an irony of fate that he should do so under such circumstances.

What he desired to do more than anything in the world was to take her into his arms, undress her and cover her with kisses, to murmur a million endearments to her.

"My dearest love. My beautiful Elizabeth."

She wasn't *his* at all. He wanted to crush her to him, tell her all the things he had dreamt of telling her, but he had no right to say them. No right to say anything at all.

Instead he managed to stammer out something, he hardly knew what, as he climbed out behind her and watched her step onto solid ground. Safe. "Miss Bennet— are you—have you been injured?"

"Mr. Darcy!! I—no, 'tis nothing—" But as she started to step out, she winced and sucked in her breath and her right knee buckled. He was instantly beside her. He lifted her off the ground despite her protests and began to carry her.

"Place your hands around my neck so I can transfer you to my carriage. It will make it easier."

Her hands against the skin of his neck were exquisite torture. He contented himself with carrying her in his arms, tenderly, so as not to injure her leg. Her face was hidden from him, buried in his coat, but her hair – abundant, thick chestnut curls, caressed the skin of his neck. He took in the scent of roses, of *her*, as deeply as he could, trying not to tremble after he had held her like this so many times in his dreams. Desire stirred in him, a hunger so deep he stumbled. His lips were close to the top of her head. He allowed them to skim her hair, to brush against her head as they moved. It was heaven to hold her close and torment, too. Only the fact that she was in pain held him back, and even that took all of his will to accomplish.

"You really don't have to carry me, Mr. Darcy," she said in her familiar teasing manner, though her voice sounded breathless. "I'm quite capable of hobbling about with just a bit of support. As long as you promise not to laugh."

Laugh? He didn't think he could laugh at this moment to save his life. He clung to her stubbornly.

"I am— perfectly capable of carrying you, Miss Bennet," he said, with an effort.

"Oh, I didn't mean to cast aspersions on your strength, Mr. Darcy, merely to remark that this show of strength is unnecessary, and might be employed to better advantage."

"You have had an accident, Miss Bennet. You may have sustained other injuries. It may also be that when the initial shock wears off you might find your legs powerless to support you."

"I assure you, my legs are quite stout enough!" She bit her lower lip. "Really. I would prefer it if you could have the cart removed so we can take my uncle to safety. And there is the coachman to see to."

Did she dislike being in his arms that much? Did she recoil from him, even under the circumstances? It was enough to try the patience of a saint, and Lord only knew he wasn't one. He steeled himself to coldness. If she did not want his assistance, then so be it.

"Very well, Miss Bennet," he said, setting her down. "You may walk the rest of the way, since you are so inclined."

Far be it for him to force his attentions on an unwilling subject.

He left her standing on one foot, arms splayed out to the sides, looking quite astonished. It gave him a savage sense of satisfaction that he had surprised her. She had not expected him to let go after all.

Her aunt was looking out of the carriage. As soon as she saw Elizabeth she hurried over to support her as she made her way to the carriage.

Every instinct of his told him that he was the one who should be helping her, in spite of her reluctance. He had to tear himself away. Now that she was here, he never wanted to let her out of his sight. His arms felt empty and cold without her. Rationally, though, he knew she was right about the cart. They needed to move quickly to clear the road in order to have a physician see to her uncle.

"Have you found our coachman?" called her aunt as he moved away.

Darcy shook his head. "I fear the worst. I am sorry. It is very possible he fell under the carriage when it overturned.

Mrs. Gardiner gave a small gasp. Elizabeth winced.

"Poor John," murmured Mrs. Gardiner.

"We won't know until we move the carriage," said Darcy, "Perhaps he was lucky enough to survive. But our first endeavor must be to clear the road. The post chaise is due soon, and we do not wish for more blood on our hands."

He did not want to let her out of his sight, not for a second, not now that he'd found her again, but time was of the essence. He did not know the extent of her uncle's injuries and he did not want to risk holding them up. Nor did he wish to delay searching for the coachman, who might still be alive. In addition, the cart was a dangerous obstacle. Any moment now a carriage would come careening down the road with disastrous consequences.

There was no time to be lost.

"Mr. Coulter, thank you for holding the horses. Now we need to move your cart out of the way as quickly as possible."

Removing the cart proved more difficult than Darcy could have imagined. Tormented by anxiety, stopping every now and then to listen for a carriage, he gritted his teeth at the seemingly insurmountable obstacles in his way. The cart was still attached to the poor animal; Mr. Coulter could not bear to unhitch it. The result was that it was left to Darcy and young Ebenezer to do so. Darcy was all urgency, but there was no speeding up matter. Unfortunately, stacked as the cart was with hay, it was too heavy to move; they were forced to remove some of the hay and pile it on the side of the road before anything could be done.

"Aye, it's easy enough to dump the hay in the road, but I don't know how I'm going to get the hay loaded back again and taken where it ought to go," said Mr. Coulter, who was no use at all, since he punctuated the little work he did with wringing his hands in consternation. "Without a pitchfork or an animal I don't know how I can do it."

"Never mind that for now, Mr. Coulter," said Darcy. "We've got an injured man in that carriage and we need to get him to a physician. I will send someone to assist you as soon as I return to Pemberley."

Finally, the cart was light enough to be moved. With Darcy pushing, Ebenezer pulling, and Mr. Coulter getting in the way, the cart was finally wheeled over to the side of the road.

There was still the original hay that had fallen in the road to be taken care of and brought to the side.

"Come on Mr. Coulter. Surely you can assist us in this at least?"

Mr. Coulter walked over slowly to the pile. As he began to lift it, muttering to himself, the hay moved. A man in livery sat up and looked around him, dazed.

"What am I doing here?" he said, looking bewildered to discover himself in the midst of the hay.

"I think we've found the missing coachman," said Darcy, biting back a mad desire to laugh, born of relief. "Thank heavens! Are you injured? Do not move until you are certain that you are not. "

With the coachman found, it meant that as soon as the road was cleared, he could go along with Elizabeth to Pemberley and he could make sure she and her family received all the care they needed.

"I will send men back to attend to your luggage and repair the carriage," Darcy said, as he stepped into the carriage and sat next to Mrs. Gardiner in the only space available, since Mr. Gardiner was lying on the opposite seat.

He had to bite down his tongue to stop himself from asking to exchange seats.

Meanwhile, he did what he could to reassure a white-faced and anxious Mrs. Gardiner that her husband would recover. He did it as much for her as for Elizabeth, who was obviously just as worried. He kept to himself the knowledge that head injuries were unpredictable, and that the sight of the uncle so still and unmoving worried him as well.

As Pemberley came into sight, he announced it, trying to keep his pride in his beautiful estate out of his voice.

"That is Pemberley across from the river. We shall be arriving in a few minutes."

He noticed Elizabeth's eyes widen as she took in the view. Perhaps now that she saw what she had given up when she turned him down, she might regret it. She could have been mistress of all this had she accepted him.

The reflection did not give him as much satisfaction as it ought. He did not particularly wish her to take him for mercenary reasons. He wanted her to desire him for himself.

He wished now he had never thought of that because now, if she did happen to change her mind, he might have to attribute it to greed.

As soon as they arrived in Pemberley, he jumped out of the carriage to summon the servant to procure a makeshift stretcher to carry the injured Mr. Gardiner, then sent for the physician, Dr. Richardson.

Mrs. Reynolds stepped forward to support Elizabeth as she walked to the doorway. It should have been him, but he did not wish to impose himself. He had dreamt so often of Elizabeth coming to Pemberley, but he could not have imagined her limping painfully into the house on Mrs. Reynolds' arm. In his visions, he had swung her over the threshold, the two of them laughing.

The reality was rather different. It began to sink in, now, that there had been an accident and Elizabeth could have been badly injured or worse.

Not wishing to pursue that thought any further, he threw himself into making sure the needs of his guests were met. He requested chambers to be prepared and went about shouting orders to anyone who was not occupied in setting things up.

It was only when Mrs. Reynolds assured him that everything that needed to be done had been done and that the new arrivals were in good hands that he allowed himself to be guided to the drawing room and served a cup of tea before going up to change.

That was when he realized that a miracle had happened.

Miss Elizabeth Bennet was back in his life. She was under his roof. She was within his reach.

He could still smell her scent on his clothes. He could still feel her body against his.

She was here, in Pemberley. It was beyond belief. He could talk to her, show her his home. He could find a way to persuade her that he was not the villain she had made him out to be.

Anything could happen now, anything at all.

For the first time in many months, Darcy allowed himself to hope.

Chapter Fourteen

The presence of a person one loves under one's roof (but not in one's bed) is not conducive to a good night's sleep. Certainly it was not in Darcy's case. He tossed and turned, turned and tossed, but the very thought that Elizabeth Bennet was just a few doorways away brought his emotions to a feverish pitch. How easy it would be to slip out of bed, steal down the corridor and slip between her sheets. To embrace her, to cover her soft skin with his kisses.

The longing to do so was so strong that Darcy could only overcome it by throwing on a shirt and trousers and tiptoeing downstairs to the library. There he did not make the mistake of trying to read. He knew that would be useless. He resisted the temptation of pouring himself a snifter – he knew he would not stop at one and he did not want to look the worse for wear the next morning. Instead, he struck a flint, lit a candle and took it to his desk. There were estate matters to be taken care of. Before he left for London his steward had given him some ledgers to look over, and he had been looking into a new irrigation method that would boost the hay yield.

When dawn arrived, he discovered himself with his cheek resting on the desk, a ledger digging into the side of his neck, the candle still lit. He groaned as he started to move, his shoulder and neck stiff from his uncomfortable position. Then he remembered Elizabeth. What if she came in and saw him in this state? He jumped up, knocking the candle over. One of the papers caught fire and in a panic he took up the paper. The flame reached out and licked at his hand, burning the delicate skin between his finger and his thumb. He threw the paper quickly to the floor and stamped on it.

The fire went out, leaving a trail of black ash on the marble floor and the smell of smoke around him.

The door opened as he knelt to pick up what was left of the burnt paper.

"There should be plenty of books for you to choose from in here, Miss Bennet," said old Butler. "When you are finished, just ring the bell and I will come and take you back to your uncle's chamber."

Darcy froze. If he stood up, Elizabeth would see him. He was in his shirt, looking completely bedraggled, with soot on his hands and undoubtedly a large red mark on his face from where he had slept on the ledger, his hair uncombed.

So much for creating a good impression.

He was tempted to stay where he was and hope that she did not come any closer. After all, as Butler had said, there were plenty of books to look at in her part of the room. From where she was in the library, she could not see him.

He moved carefully further back behind the desk. As he moved, his head brushed against a soft object. He turned to look at it.

It was the bell pull.

Butler had told her to ring the bell when she finished, and that was the only bell pull in the room.

That clinched matters, then. It was really very awkward to have to stand up now when he had not done so when she had entered, but he had no choice.

"Good morning, Miss Bennet," he said.

She was so startled that the book she was taking off the shelf slipped through her fingers and fell with a muffled thud onto the floor.

"Mr. Darcy!"

"I apologize for startling you, Miss Bennet."

He could not think of a thing to say beyond that.

He stood there, savouring every detail of her appearance – the tousled curls that had escaped their pins and had settled gently against her slender neck, the slight disarray of her fichu that revealed perhaps more than was intended of the soft rise of her chest, the dark circles that accentuated the dark brilliance of her eyes.

She stared at him as if she'd seen an apparition. No wonder. He must be barely recognizable in his state of undress. What she must think of him!

"I— did not think there would be anyone awake so early. I hope I haven't disturbed you. Do you keep country hours, then? It is very early in the morning, is it not? I have lost track of time watching over my uncle."

The mention of her uncle reminded him that there were matters of more urgent concern to her than his state of undress and he managed to gather his scattered thoughts together.

"How is your uncle? I hope he is faring better. Is he still unconscious?"

"I'm afraid so," said Elizabeth. "My aunt is very worried."

"I will send to Town today to fetch Dr. Ambrose. He is known to be good with head injuries. He may be able to help us."

"Let us hope he will have awakened soon," said Elizabeth, biting her lower lips as she was in the habit of doing.

He would have done anything to relieve her from her anxiety but he suspected there was not much anyone could do but wait.

"I will hire a woman from the village while you and your aunt get some rest. She will awaken you as soon as he stirs."

"I doubt my aunt will be able to leave his side," said Elizabeth.

"Nevertheless, she would be able to sleep a little at least if there is someone who could awaken her if there is any change."

Elizabeth nodded.

"I see your ankle is much improved," he remarked.

"Yes, it does not hurt at all," she said. "So you see, carrying me was entirely unnecessary as I pointed out yesterday. I am quite capable of walking alone."

He would not have given up that pleasure for anything.

It was only when her face turned red that he realized he had spoken the words aloud.

A ringing silence filled the room. The air seemed to crackle between them. His breath caught and he brought his hands to the desk to grip it in order to stop himself from closing the empty space that separated them and pressing his lips to hers.

"Mr. Darcy – your hands are blackened. And you have not burned yourself, have you?"

She took a step towards him and reached out to touch his hand.

Reflexively, he snatched his hand away out of her reach.

She gave him a surprised look.

He held it out. He may as well let her hold it. It throbbed with a mix of pain and anticipation. She took it and looked at it closely. He could sense everything about her – the light touch of her fingers, the soft caress of her breath against her skin, even the movement of the air as she moved. It was exquisite torture to stand there unmoving, waiting for her to complete her inspection.

"You will need to ask the physician to give you a poultice to apply on it to prevent infection," she said.

The throbbing pain from the burn intensified as she broke contact and stepped back.

"Well, Mr. Darcy, thank you for allowing me to borrow one of your books to help me wile away the time by my uncle's bedside. I assure you, we are very grateful to you for your assistance. I do not know what would have occurred if you had not happened by after the accident."

"I only wish the circumstances were a bit better." he said.

"So do I," said Elizabeth, and turned to go.

"I will see about getting a nurse to relieve you,"

"Thank you, Mr. Darcy."

"I will ring for Butler to show you the way," he said.

She gave a small smile. "No, there is no need. It is true that Pemberley is very large, but it is not so confusing as all that. I can find my way back."

And then she was gone, leaving him with the odd sensation that the morning had suddenly turned cold.

~~X~~

Darcy subjected himself to Briggs' shaving knife impatiently, and, equally impatiently, waited while the small valet fussed over his clothes.

Briggs clucked over the burn on Darcy's hand, but Darcy brushed him away under the excuse that he would have the surgeon, Mr. Mills, bind it when he came. He had asked the surgeon as well as the physician to come, in case an operation was required.

He wanted to appear at his best, of course, but he was equally worried that he would miss the physician's visit and thereby miss what he had to say about Mr. Gardiner's recovery. He was equally eager to go down and arrange for a replacement for Miss Bennet and her aunt. He did not wish her to think him remiss in his concern for her.

As it was, he arrived downstairs far too early. Dr. Richardson and the surgeon, Mr. Mills, were supposed to call at ten o'clock and it was barely past eight, so he had to content himself with speaking to Mrs. Reynolds about finding a nurse and making sure a breakfast tray was sent up to both Elizabeth and Mrs. Gardiner.

He himself was too restless to even think of eating. He downed two strong cups of coffee and went for a hard long ride.

As he rode back, he caught a glimpse of Pemberley through the leaves. It was the same building it always was, but now the sight of it evoked such a profound sense of longing it seemed ready to consume him. Knowing that his beloved Elizabeth was inside Pemberley seemed to give it an extra dimension, as if an empty structure had suddenly acquired a soul.

It felt like home.

This was what he had dreamed of, in daydreams and in the depth of night when he had awakened to discover it was not real.

The question remained: what to do about it? He had provided for every comfort, had sent her Georgiana's personal maid Jenny to wait on her, he would discover her favorite dishes and ensure that Cook provided them. These little things he could do for her. What he could not do, however, was approach her, because he was terrified he would forget himself and allow his feelings to overwhelm him. He could not bear it if he invoked in her the same feelings of disgust as he had when he had proposed. He never wanted to see that expression of disdain again on her face.

There was another possibility that he wished to avoid. He did not wish her to think she owed him a debt of gratitude for his help with the carriage accident, in which case she would dissemble and hide her distaste under a mask of politeness.

He would rather know her honest opinion of him. At least he would know exactly where he stood and he would not have any illusions.

After all, nothing had changed since that day when he had proposed. Perhaps his letter might have softened some of her preconceptions, if he had had the courage to give it to her, but he did not delude himself that it could have made her love him.

So what was he to do? Stay out of her way and leave her to nurse her uncle as best she could? Or should he make use of this time to convince her otherwise? If fate had provided this chance encounter, shouldn't he make the best of it? If it were up to his heart, he knew where his footsteps would lead, but he could not plan with his heart. He would never make that mistake again. After his disastrous proposal, he had promised himself never to do anything on impulse.

Which meant that if he wanted to win her over, he would have to keep a firm grip on his emotions and approach the whole thing rationally. He had at his disposal everything that wealth could buy, and though he knew already that such things did not signify to Elizabeth, there had to be something that would make her weaken.

The trick would be to discover what that was.

The visit of Dr. Richardson yielded nothing new. The day before, the physician had discovered that Mr. Gardiner had a broken finger. He had had mended the bone and wrapped it in a splint. But with Mr. Gardiner still unconscious, they could not determine what other injuries there may be.

"Will he recover consciousness?" asked Mrs. Gardiner, in a fearful tone.

The physician shook his head. "I cannot tell you. With head injuries, it is nigh impossible to predict recovery. We cannot see inside his head to determine the amount of injury, and symptoms of injury often do not appear until later."

The two men discussed the usefulness of trepanation, but determined it was not called for at this point.

"What is trepanation?" asked Elizabeth.

Dr. Richardson turned away, apparently unwilling to discuss the matter.

"I need to know," she said, insistently.

"It involves drilling a hole in the skull to relieve internal bleeding," said the surgeon, Mr. Mills, gently.

The ladies cringed, and even Darcy felt some trepidation at the idea.

"Is there nothing else to be done for him?" said Mrs. Gardiner.

"You must wait for him to regain consciousness," said Mr. Mills.

Or not. The words hung in the air, unsaid.

The anxiety on both women's faces prompted Darcy to accompany the physician downstairs and take him aside.

"I will spare no expense," said Darcy. "You must tell me if there is anything to be done."

"Pray," said Dr. Richardson, taking up his top hat and stick and walking through the entrance.

Mr. Mills at least proved useful by treating Darcy's burn.

A nurse arrived from the village which enabled both Elizabeth and her aunt to retire to their rooms for some rest.

Darcy consequently found himself with little to do beyond a request by Mrs. Reynolds for some fresh trout for dinner. It would be easy enough for Cook to send a boy to the fishing pond with a net, so Darcy suspected that sending him fishing was more of a ruse to keep him occupied than a real desire to include trout in this evening's menu. It had always been thus with Mrs. Reynolds. Somehow, she always knew when he was in a pickle, and clearly the years and his absences had not made her any less perceptive.

If Georgiana had been there, at least, he would have had someone to talk to, but Caroline had requested his sister's company in her carriage and they were to set out from London a day or even two later than him.

Darcy was reluctant to leave the house. He wanted to remain ensconced in the library in case Elizabeth happened to return for a book. However, there was little likelihood of that happening before she finished the book she had borrowed just a few hours ago. Moreover, she was sleeping in her room and unlikely to interrupt her much needed rest.

Unfit for doing anything else, he took out the folded piece of paper from his pocket and spread it out on the desk. It was looking tattered and blotched, with crossed out sentences and cramped writing.

He read it through, trying to remain impartial, not wanting his feelings for Elizabeth sway his purpose. He immediately reached for the quill and scratched out a quality that he had written down when in London.

A condescending attitude.

Already London seemed such a long time ago. He remembered writing the words at the time because he had been impressed by Miss Marshall's tendency to dispense her attention on those around her as if she was bestowing favors. There was a certain regal attitude to her manner that he had rather admired.

Today, however, Miss Marshall's manner seemed singularly unappealing. He was surprised, in fact, that he had ever thought her engaging. There was deception in all the arts ladies used to captivate a gentleman, but his eyes were now opened to the degree of artifice there was in Miss Marshall's conduct. Compared with Elizabeth Bennet, who was natural to a fault, Miss Marshall was a mistress of strategy.

He waited until the ink dried then folded the paper again and put it back in his pocket. He wished he could say he no longer needed it, but there was nothing in Elizabeth Bennet's behavior that would indicate she would be any more willing to accept his courtship now than she had been before.

The thought cast a pall over him.

There was nothing useful in the house for him to do. The ledgers sat waiting for him accusingly on his desk, but he had slept so little he did not think he could peruse them very accurately. He may as well oblige Mrs. Reynolds. Perhaps Elizabeth had expressed a particular desire to eat fish. He knew so little about her preferences, but he intended to find out.

At least fishing got him out of the house and gave him a purpose.

It was another glorious summer day. A flock of white clouds drifted casually across an azure sky. The scent of newly cut hay drifted towards him on the light breeze. Birds gossiped in the trees around him.

Darcy strode down from the house to the river, crossed the small bridge, and walked along the bank on the other side until he found himself a place where a large branch from the opposite bank provided shade. It was a familiar place. When his father had been alive, the two of them had often fished in this very spot.

"You see that spot where the tree roots sticks out into the water and swirls around?" said his father. "It interrupts the current. Brown trout like to gather there. That's where you need to cast."

The last time he had fished with his father had been eight years ago, a week before his father had passed away.

As he had then, Darcy pulled off his boots and stockings. Moving as quietly and carefully as possible, he stepped across the two rocks, gripping them with his toes, and onto a shallow island, making the river narrower at this point. It was a perfect location from which to cast his fly – far enough from the trees for the line not to snag on the branches, but shallow enough for him not to sink down to his knees into the water.

It was a perfect day for fishing. The water was refreshing without being too cold, the weather warm without being unpleasantly hot. The stream sparkled like ladies' jewels in a ballroom. The burble of the water relaxed his distraught senses, and he allowed himself to be lulled by it.

He cast the fly upstream and waited for the fish to take.

~~X~~

He had caught four fish and was casting the fly again when there was a loud rustle and a shout from the opposite bank.

"Mr. Darcy!"

The voice was unmistakable. It was Miss Bennet.

Taken by surprise, he stopped in mid-swing. It threw him off balance and his foot slipped.

"Oh, look out, Mr. Darcy!"

The cry had the effect of further diverting his attention as he turned to look at Elizabeth. Before he knew it, he was falling sideways towards the deeper pool in the middle of the river.

As the water rushed over him, he knew a moment's panic as the fishing line wrapped around him, entangling him so that it was difficult to move. Fortunately it was one of the old silk ones lines – they had been his father's – and he was able to break it by exerting pressure.

He pushed up to the surface in order to breathe.

"Mr. Darcy!" said Elizabeth. "Thank heavens! You were down so long I was afraid you had drowned. Here, take hold of this." She was reaching out to him with a branch.

He did not need a branch. He could swim perfectly well, and the current was not particularly strong in the summer months. However, he was not about to say no to Elizabeth Bennet, who was kneeling on the river bank leaning precariously towards him.

"Hold onto something," he said as he gasped for breath. "You don't want to fall in."

"Never mind about me," she said, anxiously. "Oh, please, do hurry!"

She was anxious for him. The possibility that she cared enough for him to be anxious warmed him up inside. In two strong strokes he reached the branch she held out and grasped it.

"Are you holding it firmly?" she said, "I'll pull you in."

She was a vision, kneeling there on the bank of his river, her face all scrunched up in concentration. He was almost tempted to splash about and pretend to drown again, if it meant having that expression of concern on her face.

Using her left arm to anchor her by wrapping it around the trunk of a tree, she slowly stood up and managed to pull him closer to the bank. She was surprisingly strong.

"Is the water shallow enough for you to stand?"

At this point it would hardly reach his waist if he stood up, but he remained submerged, enjoying every moment of her attention.

But he could not delay forever.

He lingered for a few more minutes then decided it was time to emerge.

"I believe I can stand up now," he said.

She nodded, dropped the branch and gave him her gloved hand as he waded through the water and reached the bank.

His hand was bare and wet. Within seconds, her glove was soaked and clinging to her hand. She might as well not have been wearing gloves. The contact sent shivers and such a profusion of sensations through him that he no longer knew what he was doing. He would happily have fallen back into the river at that moment.

"Mr. Darcy! You are really doing nothing to help."

He realized he was gazing at her with a puppy-dog grin on his face. *Where is your brain, Darcy? You are hardly endearing yourself to her by playing the fool.*

He scrambled up the bank with as much dignity as he could, considering she was still holding one of his hands. When he reached the top and was able to stand, she began to let his hand go, but he clung to it.

"I have to thank you, Miss Bennet, for rescuing me from the river," he said, taking up that precious gloved hand in both of his and planting a kiss on it.

The effect of this chivalrous gesture was diminished by the fact that his other hand was mud-smeared and left a dark smear on her white gloves.

He had been contemplating pulling off her glove and covering it with kisses, then making his way slowly up her arm to the hollow in her shoulder and the gentle curve of her breasts.

Luckily, the stain brought him to his senses.

"My apologies, Miss Bennet. I seem to have ruined your gloves."

"They can be washed easily enough," said Elizabeth, dismissing his qualms with a little laugh. "Besides, it is no more than I deserved. It is entirely my fault for startling you and making you fall in the river."

She colored and, withdrawing her hands from his grasp abruptly, she focused her gaze on a distant point in the landscape.

He had really not thought her dislike of him was that strong.

Then a sly sideways look of hers alerted him to the state of his clothing.

Looking downwards, he found his shirt clinging closely to his body, outlining his chest, while his nankeen breeches had turned into a second skin, leaving very little to the imagination.

He stepped back in embarrassment, and cast a quick look around him for his clothes, but naturally he had left them on the other bank.

There was a long awkward silence in which neither of them knew what to say or do.

"What was it you came here—" he began.

"I was told you would be—" she began.

"You first," they both said simultaneously.

They laughed uneasily.

It was Elizabeth who finally spoke up.

"I came here to impart my good news. My uncle has regained consciousness! So far he appears coherent, though he does not remember the accident at all."

"That is delightful news, Miss Bennet," he said, wishing he could take her in his arms, swing her around and give out a loud whoop of joy. He felt entirely graceless standing there so stiffly when something so momentous had happened. "How very fortunate! Your aunt must be in the best of spirits. Let us hope his recovery is fast."

"It is far better than I could have hoped for. He complains of dizziness and a headache if he tries to sit up, but does not seem to have suffered anything more. It seems you will not need to send for Dr. Ambrose after all. However, I am afraid we must trespass on your hospitality a little longer."

Trespass? Every moment she spent under his roof was bliss. At the thought of her leaving, his heart contracted painfully.

"You must not even consider leaving inside of a week," he said, firmly, "not until he is fully recovered and able to travel."

He would keep her there longer than that, he promised himself, but even a week was an unexpected blessing. A week would give him a chance to convince her of his virtues, or, barring that, the virtues of marrying into an estate like Pemberley.

"You are very kind, Mr. Darcy."

He was not kind at all. He was acting out of pure selfishness.

"Not at all," he said, with a bow. "In the meantime, Miss Bennet, you must avail yourself of anything you please at Pemberley. Please let Mrs. Reynolds know about your and Mrs. Gardiner's food preferences or she will fret. I do not suppose Mr. Gardiner will be equal to eating normally yet. I am expecting a party from Town tomorrow – those who will claim an acquaintance with you – Mr. Bingley and his sisters. "

Elizabeth answered only by a slight bow. He could tell her thoughts were instantly driven back to the time when Mr. Bingley's name had been last mentioned between them; Darcy cursed himself for mentioning them when he was doing everything he could to make her forget his unfortunate proposal.

"There is also one other person in the party," he continued after a pause, "who more particularly wishes to be known to you. Will you allow me, or do I ask too much, to introduce my sister to your acquaintance during your stay?"

"Of course," said Elizabeth, looking surprised.

He should not have expressed it that way. Now she would wonder what he told his sister, when he had in fact told her nothing. He would have to waylay Georgiana, somehow, and warn her to treat Miss Bennet very civilly.

"Does your sister spend much time at Pemberley?"

"She has done so lately," said Darcy. "But until a year ago she was at a young ladies' academy, and only had the opportunity to come here for her holidays."

He could see in Elizabeth's eyes that she was thinking of Ramsgate. He resisted the temptation to mention it, however.

"And the Bingleys?"

"I have known the Bingleys for many years. Bingley was with me at school, and more often than not, he used to spend the summers at Pemberley. Later, his sisters came to join him. Mr. Bingley enjoys fishing."

"My uncle enjoys fishing, too," said Elizabeth, still keeping her gaze away from him.

He could not stand here forever, half-undressed, trying to prevent her from going.

"If you will wait for me," said Darcy, "I will fetch my clothes and we can return to Pemberley together."

"Thank you, Mr. Darcy," she said, shaking her head with a small laugh. "But I would rather continue alone. Now that there is no necessity to care for my uncle, I would like to walk through the Park. I know it is considered rather odd of me to wish to traipse around the countryside, but I dearly love to walk."

"I am aware of that," said Darcy, smiling as he recalled the day she had arrived in Netherfield, her shoes coated in mud. "Do not go far, however, or you might get lost. The Park and the woods span ten miles and unless you know the grounds, you could easily mistake one path for another. I will show you and your aunt around the Park tomorrow, if you wish."

"Oh, I never get lost, Mr. Darcy," said Elizabeth, her dark eyes dancing in a most charming manner. "Have no fear. I will make sure to keep Pemberley in my sights all the time, that way I could never mistake my way. Luckily, that should not be difficult since Pemberley stands on an incline. If I am not back by three o'clock, you may send a search party for me, but I assure you it will not be necessary."

With that she set out, removing her bonnet from her head and swinging it merrily in her hand.

He resisted the temptation to warn her that the sun was quite hot and that she would be better served to keep the bonnet on her head. She would not thank him for his interference, he sensed.

He watched her go until her figure was hidden behind some trees.

Darcy went back to retrieve his clothes and his trout, cursing inwardly at the fact that, with his shirt and breeches wet and the fish likely to spoil in the heat, he could not join her in her walk. It vexed him endlessly that he had fallen in and thus deprived himself of her company.

He could only console himself with the fact that at least he would be able to spend the whole evening in her presence.

Chapter Fifteen

"You seem to be even more restless than usual tonight, Mr. Darcy, if you don't mind my saying so," said Briggs, putting the finishing touches on Darcy's carefully arranged cravat.

"No more restless than usual, Briggs," said Darcy, firmly, cutting off any possibility of discussion. Briggs had a tendency to pry, if given even the smallest hint of encouragement, and Darcy did not want this conversation to go any further.

"If you say so, sir." The little valet took out a clothes brush and began to brush Darcy's shoulders. "Although I will say it's good to have company at Pemberley again. It's been too quiet lately."

Darcy chaffed under Brigg's ministrations. It seemed to him that Briggs was taking longer than usual preparing him for dinner. He did not wish to *appear* impatient, however. It would only add fuel to Briggs' observation.

"I wouldn't call it quiet," said Darcy, itching to get away. "Miss Marshall and Lady Renwick were frequent visitors not so long ago."

"I have to say it's a relief not to have Miss Marshall here, sir," said Briggs. "She thinks she's the queen of Sheba, that one, ordering the servants here and there as if it was her own house. You're not by any chance still considering her, are you, Mr. Darcy?"

"Certainly not," said Darcy, before he had time to think.

A knowing look came into the valet's eyes.

"I thought as much, sir" he said and began to whistle a cheerful tune.

Darcy raised his eyebrow haughtily, but Briggs merely grinned.

"Miss Bennet is a pretty young lady, is she not, Mr. Darcy?" said the little valet with studied nonchalance, pulling down Darcy's sleeves to make sure there were no creases.

"Is she?" said Darcy, feigning indifference. "I have seen very little of her."

"And not likely to, sir," said the valet.

"What do you mean?" said Darcy, in alarm.

"I believe she ordered food to be taken up to her room tonight."

Darcy cursed and, pulling at the cravat that Briggs had so lovingly arranged, tore it off and threw it on the bed.

Briggs laughed. "Look what you've gone and done now, sir. We shall have to start all over again! I was only teasing you, sir. I have it on good authority that Jenny, Miss Georgiana's maid, is with her right now, dressing her hair."

"That was a dastardly trick to play on me, Briggs," said Darcy, coldly, annoyed that he had been trapped into revealing his feelings. "You may leave now. I shall take care of tying my cravat myself."

"Not on your life, Mr. Darcy," said the valet. "I will not have you appearing downstairs looking anything but your best, sir. Even if Miss Elizabeth does not come down to dinner, there is still Mrs. Gardiner to consider."

"One day, Briggs," said Darcy, "I am going to strangle you with one of my cravats."

"You are forgetting, Mr. Darcy, that I hold a blade to your throat each morning," said the little man. "Should the blade happen to slip just a little—"

Darcy took up a cushion from the chair in front of him and threw it at the laughing valet. It missed, crashing into the mirror instead. Fortunately, the mirror did not break.

Briggs shook his head with mock disapproval. "Supposing Miss Bennet were passing by right now and heard you throwing objects across the room," he said. "It would not give too good of an impression now, would it, sir?"

Darcy did not deem the remark worthy of an answer. Instead, he checked his appearance in the mirror, smoothed back a lock of hair and, with exaggerated dignity, strode from the room.

~~X~~

Darcy was in the drawing room even before the gong for dinner sounded. He had arrived unfashionably early, something he would never have been guilty of doing in Town, but, confound it, this was his home and he had the right to be early if he wished!

There was only one downside to it—it meant he had to wait for the others to join him.

If he kept country hours like most people in Derbyshire instead of following the dictates of the fashionable set, then they would have been at dinner some time ago.

He wandered over to the French windows and stepped out, snifter in hand. At first he contemplated the high woody hills behind the house, but his gaze was soon drawn down to the river where he had met with Elizabeth earlier. That spot would forever be associated with her in his mind.

It was taking forever for the gong to sound. Was it possible that old Timmons had forgotten the time? Every day since he had been a child, someone had struck the gong to announce dinner and for most of his life, it had been Timmons, but the butler was growing older. It was entirely probable that he had not remembered.

Darcy grew so convinced of this that he went out in search of Mrs. Reynolds. Just then, the sonorous gong echoed through the house.

"Is there something wrong, Mr. Darcy? Anything I can help with?" said Timmons, no doubt wondering why the master had come in search of someone rather than using the bell.

"No, nothing," said Darcy. "I had a question for Mrs. Reynolds, but it is of no importance."

"I would be happy to send her up, sir," said Timmons.

"Really, there is no need."

Darcy beat a hasty retreat into the drawing room, avoiding the curious looks of two footmen who were carrying candles into the dining hall.

If he continued in this manner, the kitchen would be awash with gossip before the end of the evening. He really had to find a way to calm his nerves.

It was only a dinner, after all.

But logic failed to take hold. Inside his gloves, the palms of his hands were moist. Surreptitiously, hoping no one would come in and see him, he took the gloves off and wiped them on his breeches, then put them painstakingly on, finger by finger.

The process did while away some time, but not nearly enough.

Then finally there were footsteps on the staircase and he turned towards the door, his heart bumping against his ribs like a bird trying to escape its cage.

At first he did not recognize her. He thought his eyes were playing tricks on him. The lady who entered was the height of elegance. Her hair had been piled up like a crown into a braid which weaved through a demi-turban, exposing her long neck. The blue satin robe was gathered tantalizingly tight around the bodice and Darcy had to look away to avoid the temptation of staring at the rounded curves outlined so clearly by the material. The white satin slip under her robe fell in soft angelic folds to the ground and her flame-colored tunic, all the rage in London, floated behind her like wings.

Was this Elizabeth, or was it an unknown beauty who drifted towards him? He stood frozen in place, trying to reconcile this apparition with the simply dressed young lady he had known at Rosings.

"Good evening, Mr. Darcy."

Somehow, he managed to tear his eyes from the vision and notice that the lady behind the vision was smiling at him a little uncertainly, waiting for him to acknowledge her.

Mrs. Gardiner. Of course. She probably thought he was snubbing her.

He came to his senses, cleared his throat, and bowed to the two ladies, who curtseyed back.

"Mrs. Gardiner. Miss Bennet. Forgive me. I was woolgathering."

A relieved smile appeared on Mrs. Gardiner's face.

"An apt phrase in this area, given the prevalence of sheep in the pastures," said Mrs. Gardiner, her eyes twinkling.

He turned to Elizabeth. "Did you enjoy your walk, Miss Bennet?"

"Very much," said Elizabeth, smiling broadly. "I quite forgot myself, and have become quite ruddy as a consequence of being out so long in the sun. I don't regret a moment of it, however. The landscape here is sublime."

His heart swelled at hearing her opinion of his estate. This is what he had hoped for. If she could not love him, at least she could be swayed by love of his land.

"I am glad you find it pleasant."

"More than pleasant, I assure you, Mr. Darcy."

A pause followed.

"How is Mr. Gardiner faring?" said Darcy. "I will look in on him later, but I hope he is faring well."

"He is mending slowly – far, far better than I had hoped. What a relief it was to have him open his eyes! I do not think I was ever as happy in my life as that moment." Mrs. Gardiner's eyes sparkled with unshed tears. "I wish I knew how to thank you, Mr. Darcy, for coming to our rescue as you did. I do not know what would have happened if you had not come along."

The sincerity in Mrs. Gardiner's gratitude made him feel humble.

"Someone else would have come along, Mrs. Gardiner," he said, coloring slightly, conscious of Elizabeth's gaze.

"But they would all have been strangers, which would have been much more awkward," said Elizabeth. "Now we at least have the comfort of a prior acquaintance."

So she felt comfortable around him. That, at least, was something to hold onto.

"Allow me to compliment you on your dress, Miss Bennet. I have not seen you wear it before, I believe."

He had the satisfaction of seeing Elizabeth discomfited.

"I do so like a young man who notices what ladies wear," exclaimed Mrs. Gardiner. "All too often men do not pay the least attention."

"I only notice when a lady's natural beauty is enhanced by what she wears," said Darcy, looking at Elizabeth to make sure she knew the remark was intended for her. "I admit I am not fond of frills and flounces and all the things that young ladies, including my sister, seem able to talk about for hours. But I do appreciate when a lady's clothes indicate her refinement."

"Unfortunately I can't claim all the credit, Mr. Darcy," replied Elizabeth. "It was my aunt who nudged me towards buying this dress."

"Then I must bow to Mrs. Gardiner's good taste."

He could tell that his civility took Elizabeth by surprise. Good. If he could bring her to revise her opinion just a little every day, then by the end of the week she would be forced to reconsider her harsh assessment of his character.

At this moment, a footman arrived to announce dinner. Darcy chaffed at the rules that required him to escort Mrs. Gardiner into the dining hall rather than Elizabeth, simply because she was married. Even when the London party arrived and Mr. Gardiner improved sufficiently to join them, he would still have no opportunity to take Elizabeth's arm.

He was intensely aware of her close behind him. All his senses were heightened by the knowledge. He could feel the air move as she stepped forward – hear the rustle of her dress against her thighs as she moved – breathe in the subtle scent of rosewater.

As she took the seat to his left, she was close enough for his knee to rub accidentally against hers as he was seated. He did not look at her, pretended he did not notice, but the contact sent a delicious shiver through him. He had never liked the kind of ploys others seemed to enjoy so much – touching under the table held no appeal – he had always considered them childish, but now he was almost physically compelled to do it, and he had to struggle to stop himself.

"It grows darker much later here than in the south," remarked Mrs. Gardiner. "Yesterday the sun did not set until past ten o'clock. I find it rather disorienting."

He groaned inwardly. Was he expected to keep up a stream of idle chit-chat all through dinner? He was not good at it at the best of times, and now with Elizabeth here to distract him, he did not think he could get two words out. If only he was one of those men who could impress her with his wit and charming conversation.

"The advantage, of course, is that I can read until late without straining my eyes," said Elizabeth, continuing the conversation. "It is such a relief not to need candles."

Here was his opportunity to look at her – the long dark eyelashes framing her eyes, the gentle slope of her nose, the soft mold of her mouth—

"—would you not agree, Mr. Darcy?"

He had missed what she had said.

He cleared his throat. "Of course."

Mrs. Gardiner's gaze was upon him, questioning. He shifted uncomfortably. This was not how he had envisioned the evening with Elizabeth at all. There would be no opportunity to talk, to get to know her, to charm her. Under the scrutiny of Mrs. Gardiner, he faced a long dreary dinner knowing Elizabeth was next to him but unable to say a single personal word to her. It was an ordeal. He wished for an interruption – anything to free him from the constraints upon him.

He cleared his throat. "Your parents are in good health, Miss Bennet?"

"Yes indeed. At least, they were when I left them."

"And all your sisters?"

"They are all in good health."

"Good."

"How long were you planning to stay in Derbyshire, Mrs. Gardiner? Did you have a particular destination in mind?"

"Our plan was to tour the area for about a month, our destination was the Peaks," her face fell. "That was before the accident, of course."

"Let us hope he will recover sufficiently to make at least a short tour possible," said Darcy. "What brought you to this area?"

Was it possible Elizabeth had specifically asked to see Pemberley?

"I wanted to stop in Lambton for a few days," explained Mrs. Gardiner, "Or we would not have come this way. I passed four years in the village and I have happy memories. I still have friends here I wished to see."

"I see," said Darcy, with a sense of crushing disappointment. It would have given him hope to know that Elizabeth had expressed a wish to see Pemberley. "If you would like the carriage to go into Lambton to meet your friends, you must tell Timmons. I will leave instructions with him."

Mrs. Gardiner beamed at him. "That is most generous of you, sir. The repairs to our carriage are not yet completed, so your offer is very much appreciated. I would like to go into the village. As long as Mr. Gardiner is doing well, I might slip into the village for an hour or two tomorrow."

"Perhaps I may accompany you, aunt," said Elizabeth.

"No," said Darcy. He wanted her to stay in Pemberley. Then realizing how arrogant that sounded, he corrected himself. "My sister should be arriving tomorrow morning. I would particularly like you to meet her."

"Well, then," said Mrs. Gardiner, "I am sure you will have an opportunity to meet my friends another day, Lizzy."

There was a pause in the conversation in which everyone tried to think of what to say.

"I see your bruise is beginning to fade, Mrs. Gardiner. Have you sustained any other injuries?"

"A few knocks and bruises that are already healing. We were fortunate the accident was no worse."

"Most certainly. People have been more grievously injured in far lesser situations. How is Mr. Gardiner faring?"

"He continues to improve, but unfortunately – or perhaps fortunately, he has lost all memory of the event. It is very disorienting for him, poor man, but I daresay he will become accustomed to it in time. If that is the only impact – that and the broken finger -- then we must consider ourselves blessed."

"Most definitely, madam. It is a far better outcome than anyone could have expected."

"Indeed," said Elizabeth. "I can scarcely believe I escaped with no more than a mildly sore ankle and a small cut on my head."

149

"Is your ankle recovered?"

It was a well-turned ankle. He had caught a good glimpse of it when he had lifted her from the carriage.

"Well enough for me go for a long walk," said Elizabeth, her eyes twinkling, "which is all I care about."

"What about the cut?"

"It will take a few days to heal."

"May I see it? It may require the physician's attention," said Darcy.

"It has been artfully hidden by a braid," said Elizabeth, laughing. "I cannot undo my hair to show you the cut, but I assure you, it is nothing serious."

He swallowed as the thought of her undoing her hair brought unwanted images into his head.

Control yourself. Say something charming instead of gawking like a schoolboy.

"I would certainly not wish to destroy such an artful hairstyle. It becomes you well."

Awkward, but better than nothing.

"Thank you, Mr. Darcy. I have your sister's maid to thank for it."

There was a long silence in which he tried to think of something witty or charming to say. Nothing came to mind.

He was failing in his aim. How could he charm her into liking him when he could barely string together a sentence?

The evening was dragging on interminably, yet he did not want it to end. He was no good at polite conversation. Mrs. Gardiner was gracious and helpful, but he wished she was not there.

He had been so looking forward to dinner this evening, but he had forgotten the old adage. *Two's company, three's a crowd.* If only there were more people, it would be far easier to have a regular conversation.

Just then, there was the sound of more than one carriage drawing up to the front.

Darcy smiled and came to his feet at once. His prayer had been answered.

"I do believe my sister and her party have arrived already. Pray continue with your dinner while I attend to our guests."

The London party had come early. He had not expected them until tomorrow. He would never have thought so, but they were the answer to his prayers. Now, with so many people around, surely he would get the chance to speak to Elizabeth alone?

Dishes were sent back to the kitchen to be warmed. The new arrivals were invited to join them at the dinner table. Everyone made conversation, but as Mrs. Hurst replaced Mrs. Gardiner and Mrs. Gardiner replaced Elizabeth, Darcy could no longer hope for intimate conversation with her. Mr. Bingley was eager to speak to Elizabeth; he had many questions about her sisters, though he dared not allude to any particular one. He was cordial and friendly in his usual unassuming manner and the excitement of everyone's arrival, the chaos it created in the kitchens, the unusual manner of being seated at a dinner that had already begun all made the atmosphere completely different from the silent tension earlier.

Elizabeth was much more animated now, speaking to Mr. Bingley. If Darcy could not speak to her much, he could at least observe her. As a consequence his eyes strayed to her constantly, until he realized Miss Bingley was looking at him quizzingly.

"It has been a very long time since I have had the pleasure of seeing you last," said Bingley. "It is above eight months. We have not met since the 26th of November, when we were all dancing together at Netherfield."

"Your memory is very good, Mr. Bingley," said Elizabeth. "My sister Jane was in London for some time earlier this year. Did you not have the opportunity of meeting her?"

Bingley's expression darkened. "Unfortunately I was unaware that she was there until much later."

Darcy looked away. He remembered only too well that Jane's presence in London, and Bingley's ignorance of it, had precipitated Elizabeth's rejection of him.

"Pray, Miss Eliza," said Caroline, breaking into the conversation. "Are not the Militia removed from Meryton? They must be a great loss to *your* family. I believe Wickham was a strong favorite."

Darcy did not know where to look. A cursory glance at Georgiana revealed that she was shifting in her seat, her eyes averted, staring into her plate. Darcy knew the unexpected question was intended as a slight to Elizabeth, but it brought back so many unpleasant recollections he needed time to master his emotions.

"Yes, I believe the Militia has moved to Brighton," Elizabeth answered in a tolerably disengaged tone. "Meryton will be all the quieter without their presence. They are often so lively one scarcely remembers that their role is to protect us in case of invasion from France."

Elizabeth's collected behavior soon quieted Darcy's sentiments, and Georgiana recovered sufficiently to turn to the person next to her to make a remark about London.

Thank heavens at least one of them had kept her head.

His hand went to his pocket and the little paper inside. He could tick off one major trait on his list because it certainly applied to Elizabeth.

Keeping calm and collected in a pickle.

"Well, Darcy, you certainly have all the luck!" murmured Bingley, after the ladies had left the gentlemen to their port. "I only wish Jane Bennet had been travelling with her sister!"

Darcy nodded agreement. It was a blessing he could never have expected.

"That is why I must make the best of it. I feel I have been given a second opportunity. If I do not grab it with both hands I would be the biggest fool alive. I hope you will help me find opportunities to talk to Miss Bennet without interference."

"I say, Darcy, must you whisper in the corners with Bingley? Are we going to play a decent card game tonight?" interrupted Mr. Hurst. "I hope you do not intend to make us listen to the ladies singing all night. The caterwauling always sends me to sleep."

Darcy turned away from Bingley and replied cheerfully.

"Fear not, Hurst. You shall have your game."

Card games would keep everyone occupied. He hoped that, as she had done at Netherfield, Elizabeth would refuse to play, which would in turn give him the opportunity to speak to her.

To his bitter disappointment, however, when the gentlemen rejoined the ladies a few minutes later, Mrs. Gardiner and Elizabeth had both retired already, having determined that they needed to spend some time with Mr. Gardiner who was undoubtedly in need of some amusement.

Mr. Hurst headed immediately in the direction of the card-table to set up a game of loo and gestured to Bingley and the others to join him. As they took their seats, Darcy hesitated. He would much rather have gone to see how Mr. Gardiner was doing.

"I hope you intend to play with us, Mr. Darcy," cried Caroline.

It would have been uncivil to refuse, but he would have been far better off doing so because the moment he had been dealt his cards, Miss Bingley began immediately to speak of Elizabeth.

"How very ill Eliza Bennet looked tonight, Mr. Darcy," she said; "I never in my life saw any one so much altered as she is since the winter. She is grown so brown and coarse! Louisa and I were agreeing that we should not have known her again."

Mrs. Hurst nodded agreement and added. "I have always been of the opinion that there is something wild about her."

Today Darcy had no patience for either Caroline or Louisa's snide remarks. Normally, he brushed them aside indifferently, knowing there was no harm in them, but when the object of their remarks was Elizabeth, it was difficult not to find offence in them.

"I have noticed no alteration in her except that she is rather tanned, which is no miraculous consequence of travelling in the summer."

"For my own part," Caroline rejoined, "I must confess that I never could see any beauty in her. Her face is too thin; her complexion has no brilliancy; and her features are not at all handsome. Her nose wants character -- there is nothing marked in its lines. Her teeth are tolerable, but not out of the common way; and as for her eyes, which have sometimes been called so fine, I never could perceive anything extraordinary in them. They have a sharp, shrewish look, which I do not like at all; and in her air altogether there is a self-sufficiency without fashion, which is intolerable."

Darcy did not care for Caroline's assessment of his beloved Elizabeth, but he remained resolutely silent. He had only just made friends again with Charles after their disagreement; he did not wish to quarrel with Caroline as well. He had known her since she was a little girl in pigtails. But as she continued in the same manner for some time, he found himself growing more and more nettled by her persistence in disparaging the woman he loved.

"I remember, when we first knew her in Hertfordshire, how amazed we all were to find that she was a reputed beauty; and I particularly recollect your saying one night, after they had been dining at Netherfield, 'She a beauty! I should as soon call her mother a wit.' But afterwards she seemed to improve on you, and I believe you thought her rather pretty at one time."

"Yes," replied Darcy, who could contain himself no longer, "but that was only when I first knew her; for it is many months since I have considered her as one of the handsomest women of my acquaintance."

Rather than make an exhibition of his feelings, Darcy put down his cards with a quick laugh, saying something about having the worst luck in the world in cards, pushed back his chair and excused himself by saying he had forgotten to give his valet specific instructions about his clothing, and quietly left the room.

Chapter Sixteen

Pemberley had come alive. That was Darcy's first thought next morning upon hearing Elizabeth's voice as he heard her speaking to his sister. He had requested Georgiana to be particularly civil to Elizabeth and Mrs. Gardiner, explaining the ordeal they had gone through and Georgiana, gentle soul that she was, was clearly expending the effort to make Elizabeth feel welcome. Eventually, he would tell Georgiana about Elizabeth, but he felt too shy to speak about it now, particularly since Elizabeth was here. He could become too self-conscious with his sister watching; it was already bad enough with Bingley commenting on his every move.

He grinned and rubbed his hands together. Like himself, Elizabeth was clearly an early riser. Bingley and his sisters, on the other hand, would sleep until much later. Since both Elizabeth and Georgiana were already up and about, he had a perfect opportunity. He would go down and offer his services as a guide on a walking tour of the grounds.

Hardly had he began his descent of the stairs, however, when a carriage drew up to the entrance.

Darcy frowned. Who could it be? They were not expecting anyone else.

"Who is it, Timmons?" he said, as the old butler straightened his coat and puffed out his chest in preparation. It must be someone important if Timmons was assuming his most dignified stance – a stance he reserved for only two visitors.

Darcy groaned.

"Lord and Lady Matlock, sir," said the old butler, preparing to step out to receive them.

Darcy's first impulse was the cowardly one which was to run, but it would serve only to delay the meeting, not to escape it. His pipedream of an idyllic morning spent strolling with Elizabeth through Pemberley Park dissipated into thin air.

So like Timmons, he straightened his clothes and tried to look as dignified as he could as he bowed to the inevitable – and to Lord and Lady Matlock.

"Welcome to Pemberley, Uncle. Lady Matlock. To what do I owe this unexpected pleasure?"

"You may well ask," said Lord Matlock. "Come inside, and all will be revealed."

Several trunks were being unloaded from the carriage – with Lady Matlock occupied in giving instructions to several of the footmen who were running about trying to do their best to please her.

Darcy's heart sank. The trunks, surely, were the sign of a prolonged stay, which would make the possibility of time alone with Elizabeth much more difficult to achieve.

"Darcy, you really must get married soon," said Lady Matlock. "I suppose I will have to give instructions for dinner to the housekeeper myself."

"If you tell Georgiana what it is you would wish, I am sure she can pass on her instructions."

"Ah, yes, Georgiana." Lord Matlock looked around. "Where is the gal? She should be here to welcome us."

"She is otherwise occupied, Uncle. I am afraid you have arrived at an awkward time. We have a party of guests staying for the moment."

"Not awkward at all, Darcy. There is nothing I like better than a house party. But business first and pleasure later."

He looked towards Lady Matlock. "Shall I do the honors, or do you wish to do so, my dear?"

"It was you who arranged everything. It is only right that you should take credit for your *coup*."

"Very well, then. The news is that none other than the Duke of Bolton – the duke himself – has expressed interest in marrying your sister. Naturally, I told him you were her guardian and that he needed to speak to you. However, that is a mere formality. He is a friend of mine and a man of his word. You will need to do nothing beyond escorting our dear Georgiana to Hurlstone to meet the duke." Lord Matlock clapped

Darcy on the shoulder. "You cannot imagine how relieved we are; we could not endure the idea of Georgiana dwindling into an old maid, her beauty coming to nothing."

"Even though you were rather naughty, Darcy, and did not have her miniature taken as we requested." Lady Matlock wagged her finger at him with mock seriousness.

"There has scarcely been time—" began Darcy.

"Fortunately," the Earl interrupted, "it makes no difference, for he has agreed to have her, sight unseen. I have described her looks to him, and he has been exceedingly accommodating. 'I have complete faith in you, Matlock,' he said. 'If you say the chit is handsome enough, then I will take your word for it. Of course, she may be young and half-baked enough to desire a meeting before we draw up the betrothal papers. I am willing to indulge her in that.'"

"Needless to say," said Lady Matlock. "We hurried here at once to make sure such an opportunity does not slip from our hands."

"Precisely," said Lord Matlock. "Bolton is not known for his patience. He is a man of action, and when he resolves on a thing, it must happen at once. We must leave for his estate with all haste."

"Think of it, Darcy," said Lady Matlock. "A duke in the family! What a triumph! Never in her wildest dreams could Georgiana have imagined such an honor. Have her prepare her trunks immediately. We will leave first thing in the morning. I hope you have not been neglecting her clothing and that she has appropriate outfits at hand. They need not be the latest mode. The Duke will not be particular about *that*, I assure you. He is a very generous gentleman and will be more than willing to provide her with a wardrobe befitting a duchess. And she need not be afraid he will hide her away in the country. He is keen to display her in town. He is one of Prinny's set, you know – very well connected."

Darcy was so seized with horror that he sat silently listening to his uncle and aunt prattle on. He blamed himself for not having put an end to this ridiculous charade. He had been distracted with other matters, and had never sent a reply to their letter as he ought to have done.

He had really not thought it would come to this.

"Well, Darcy. What are you waiting for?"

"You must understand that it is impossible for me to abandon my house guests at such short notice. Besides, I already made myself quite clear, Uncle, that I did not intend to marry Georgiana at such a young age."

"She is hardly young, Darcy. She is soon to be seventeen. Compared to my daughters, that is an *advanced* age. Why, she is practically on the shelf compared to them."

Darcy tried to approach the matter tactfully.

"Lady Matlock, your daughters could be married at a young age because they had the advantage of your wise council and they were prepared to take up their duties as mistresses in grand households. Georgiana, however, having lost her mother, has lacked such instruction. She is only now beginning to learn those tasks which being away at school has delayed considerably. In addition, she is naturally shy, and finds herself often tongue-tied in company. She would make a poor wife."

"Stuff and nonsense," said his uncle. "I am sure Bolton's mother would be quite happy to instruct her on what she needs to learn before removing to the Dowager house."

"Allow me to be the judge of what Georgiana is capable or not capable of doing. I can assure you that it would be unwise for her to marry."

Lady Matlock stared at him as if he had told her the world was made of cheese.

"My dear Darcy," she said. "I do not think you realize the import of what is happening. Since you were a boy, I always felt you had your head in the clouds – far too full of fanciful ideas. Why, I even remember you once declaring that the pillars of the house were some imaginary Greek monster." She laughed. "Do you remember that, Matlock?"

Lord Matlock guffawed. "I certainly do. Such fanciful ideas. You must face reality, my boy, *reality*. One cannot live in a fantasy world forever."

"I was only ten years old at the time, Uncle, and it was Atlas, a Greek god, not a monster," said Darcy, annoyed that they would even think of bringing that up now. "But that is neither here nor there. It has nothing to do with the subject at hand. The fact is, I am Georgiana's guardian," he continued, "and I have no intention of handing over a young lady barely out of childhood to a shriveled up old man just because he happens to be a Duke."

Lady Matlock gave a gasp and began to fumble in her reticule. "Where are my smelling salts!" she cried. "Oh, to be subjected to something like this! I have never heard anything like it! Where is your respect for tradition? For the best of what our country has to offer? One would think he was raised by French revolutionaries. Next, I suppose, you will crying for the guillotine to be chopping the nobility's heads off."

"Shame on you, Darcy," said Lord Matlock. "I always warned your father not to let you run around with a mere steward's son – that it would give you the wrong notion of class – but he would have none of it. 'It will do the lad good to learn to deal with those less fortunate than himself,' he said. I only regret that he is not alive today to see the consequences."

Lady Matlock had taken out her smelling salts and was holding them under her nose, looking as if she would faint any moment. "Precisely," she managed to gasp. "How convenient for him that he died without having to face the outcome of his folly."

"Quite," said Lord Matlock. "And besides, I must object to having the duke referred to as a shriveled old man. He is only a few years older than I am, and you can hardly call *me* a shriveled old man." Lord Matlock puffed out his chest and looked quelling.

"I would not, sir," said Darcy, "but I stand my ground. I am afraid you must excuse me. I will write a letter of apology immediately."

"The Duke will take your refusal as a personal insult."

"I am sorry, but I do not think it possible to insult a man I have not even had the pleasure of meeting, and who has never set eyes on me or on my sister – not when I explain the circumstances to him."

159

"But *I* have met the Duke, and I assure you, he will be exceedingly displeased."

"Never mind the duke," said Lady Matlock. "*I* am exceedingly displeased."

"I apologize, but I must withdraw to write the Duke an express at once. Meanwhile, I will hope you will take the opportunity to refresh yourself in your rooms. I will send someone to take you up."

And with that, he hurried from the room, berating himself bitterly for his lack of judgment in thinking that the Matlocks could be helpful to him in any way.

~~X~~

Georgiana had high expectations of making friends with Elizabeth Bennet. The moment she had met her, she had felt instantly at ease, and, even if her brother had not instructed her to pay particular attention to Miss Bennet, she would have felt drawn to her.

She made a particular effort to seek her out after breakfast. When she asked one of the footmen if they had seen her, they pointed her to the rose garden where Georgiana found her sitting in the sun on a bench, reading a book. To her surprise, it was not long before Caroline appeared, stopping every now and then to examine one of the roses and to stare hopefully at the entrance to the house.

"You are up unusually early, Caroline," said Georgiana with a smile.

"Whatever do you mean, Georgiana? I generally like to keep country hours when in the country and town hours when in town. I find the fresh country air inspires me to rise early."

Georgiana thought it wise to refrain from comment, but she had known Caroline a long time and was aware that Caroline never woke up early if she could help it.

"I see Miss Bennet is with a book, as usual."

"Do you often enjoy reading, Miss Bennet?" asked Georgiana, taking a seat next to her.

"Miss Bennet prefers reading to anything else," answered Caroline. "If you had her choose between a ball and a book, she would no doubt choose a book."

"Is that true, Miss Bennet?" said Georgiana. "Then you and I have something in common. I too would much rather read a book than attend a ball, but that is because I am very nervous about attending any event that has a great many strangers staring at you and whispering behind your back."

Elizabeth smiled and squeezed Georgiana's hand. "You must not worry about it, Miss Darcy. Balls only appear frightening when you have never been to one. Once you have, I am sure you will be far too caught up in meeting handsome young gentlemen to care whether anyone is whispering or staring. Shall I tell you a secret? Despite Miss Bingley's belief that you must choose one or the other, one is perfectly able to enjoy both a good book and a good ball."

Caroline was not satisfied with this answer. She opened up her parasol with a snap.

"It is unpleasantly warm this morning, is it not? I did not think to bring a fan. I do not know how Miss Eliza can bear to sit in the sun without a parasol."

"I enjoy the sensation of the sun on my skin," said Elizabeth, putting down her book and smiling lazily, "I enjoy rain, too. Being outdoors is infinitely appealing to me, particularly in a beautiful location such as this."

"It is very pretty here in Pemberley, is it not?" said Georgiana, shyly. "I have always thought it the most beautiful place in the world."

"The gardens are impressively cultivated," said Caroline, "but what are rocks and trees compared to men? I prefer people to verdure, civilization to wilderness."

"It is the rocks and trees that will endure, however, while men live their short lives and die," said Elizabeth.

"I did not know you were a philosopher as well," said Caroline, with a half-sneer.

Either Caroline did not like Elizabeth or she was expressing her frustration that Darcy had not yet proposed, Georgiana decided. More likely the latter. Bingley had shown a remarkable lack of tact when they had stopped on their way to Pemberley to change horses at an inn. She had overheard them talking from inside the carriage. Bingley questioned Caroline's impatience to be back on the road. When Caroline had replied that she was in a hurry because she expected Darcy to offer for her, Bingley had laughed in her face.

Which was not very amiable of him, thought Georgiana, but then he had no idea that Darcy had done nothing to dispel her misapprehension.

"Are you not being rather fanciful?" Bingley had remarked.

Caroline had given Bingley a complacent glance. "Why not? He would be willing enough to consider you as a husband for Georgiana."

"It is a different matter entirely."

Georgiana did not really see how it was different. She was intrigued by the possibility, however. Did Darcy really wish her to marry Bingley? She would not mind, but if Darcy was planning something like that, why had he been so particular to choose a wife who could assist with her Season? It was difficult to imagine marrying Bingley. He was more like a second brother to her than a possible husband.

The conversation seemed to have ended there, but then, as she, Louisa and Caroline had entered the front carriage, Bingley had put a hand on Caroline's shoulder to hold her back.

"Caroline, you would be well advised not to set your sights on Darcy any more," he had remarked, quite gently this time.

Clearly her brother's words had affected Caroline, since she had been out of sorts the rest of the way, leaving Georgiana and Louisa to keep up what little conversation there was. Clearly Caroline's bad humor had not dissipated yet, probably because Darcy had paid her no attention last night. Now she was taking it all out on Miss Bennet.

"I often think about how long trees live compared to us," said Georgiana, trying to take the sting out of Caroline's comment about philosophy. "I sometimes wish they could speak – I fancy they would have a great deal to tell us."

Caroline twirled her umbrella and yawned. "I have no interest in trees precisely because they have nothing to say to us. But, enough of that. I have not seen your brother this morning, Miss Darcy. I expected him to be out here mingling with his guests. I do declare he has abandoned us completely. It is really too bad of him to leave us high and dry like this."

"I certainly don't feel abandoned," said Miss Bennet. "I am doing several things I love. I am enjoying the outlook over the lawn to the valley. I am surrounded by beautiful flowers, I am reading an amusing book, and I am enjoying good company. Besides, as I am not intimately acquainted with Pemberley, I feel quite impatient to discover its nooks and crannies."

She gave Georgiana a little wink, and Georgiana couldn't help smiling back. She had taken a strong liking to Miss Bennet. There was a mixture of light heartedness and understanding in her that was very appealing. She made one feel instantly at ease.

"I have every expectation – how shall I put it delicately – of being even more intimately acquainted with Pemberley than I am currently," announced Caroline.

"Really?" said Miss Bennet, casting a glance towards Georgiana, who was feeling so mortified she did not know where to look. "Through your brother?"

Caroline's looked self-satisfied. "Certainly not. In what way can this possibly concern my brother?"

"I assumed—" Miss Bennet looked towards Georgiana again. Georgiana was surprised that someone who was only briefly introduced to the Bingleys seemed to know so much about them. Obviously she, too, seemed to think there was a plan to bring Bingley and Georgiana together. "I see I was mistaken. Now I am intrigued about your statement."

"I will say no more," said Caroline, with a mysterious air, knowing she had captured Elizabeth's attention. "Suffice it to say that I am in anticipation of a happy event occurring in the near future."

Georgiana could not believe that Caroline was hinting that Darcy intended to marry her, particularly after Bingley had specifically told her it was not likely. Even if it were the case, it was not exactly appropriate to speak of it until Darcy actually had actually proposed, which, Georgiana sensed, was far from definite at this point. It would not do for Caroline to start spreading rumors. Searching desperately for a way to turn the conversation to other matters, Georgiana wished she was more skilled at handling these kind of social situations.

"Oh, look! A skylark!" she said excitedly. "Oh, I do hope it sings."

Both ladies turned in the direction to which she pointed.

The skylark did indeed sing, a lengthy, fluid warble, but neither of the ladies paid it much attention. Miss Bennet was occupied with kicking gravel with her half-boot, and Caroline, completely unaware of what she was doing, had stopped protecting herself from the sun and was fanning herself with an open parasol in small rapid movements.

Georgiana was at a loss to understand the source of their animosity. They did not know each other well. As far as she could gather, they had met when Bingley had taken Netherfield, and had seen each other several times, but not enough for them to have taken such a dislike to each other.

Unless Miss Bennet, too, had somehow contrived the carriage accident to throw herself at Darcy. It would not be the first time that a young woman would employ desperate measures to capture a rich gentleman.

No, it could not be. Miss Bennet did not strike her as a mercenary type.

Still, if there was any kind of nascent relationship developing between Miss Bennet and her brother – he had been particularly eager to have Georgiana pay special attention to her and the Gardiners – she did not want anything to ruin it.

Reluctant as she was to leave Caroline and Miss Bennet alone together, Georgiana felt it was crucial for William to clear up matters with Caroline one way or the other before it was too late.

Chapter Seventeen

Darcy was sealing the letter of clarification he intended to send to the Duke of Bolton when Lady Matlock threw open the door and without a by-your-leave, marched into the room, followed by Lord Matlock, who sauntered in with studied arrogance, straightening the lace on his cuffs.

"I must tell you, Darcy, I take exception to your house guests," began his aunt, settling into the large leather armchair. "I know you've been a friend of that Bingley person since you were at school and felt obliged to take him under your wing for reasons I have never comprehended – all very well and good, but you *must* consider Georgiana. Surely you do not wish to expose her to the risk of falling in love with a young man who smells of trade from a mile off? The Bingleys may appear elegant – I am willing to acknowledge that – but they move in entirely different circles from us."

Smell of trade? Bingley had never engaged in trade in his life. There was no person less able to go about it if his whole future depended on it. Bingley was the most loyal of friends, and the most amiable. Rather than finding a match between Georgiana and Bingley undesirable, Darcy had in fact hoped for a match between them. Bingley would have made his sister an excellent husband – if it had not been for the circumstance of Bingley falling in love with someone else. Darcy knew better than to mention this, however. He held his tongue. He knew from experience that there was no reasoning with the Fitzwilliam side of his family. They rarely changed their opinions about anything.

"You have hit the nail on the head, my dear." Lord Matlock perused his hair in the mantle mirror and carefully dusted some powder off his hair. "It won't do to have us all under the same roof. Not the done thing at all. You have to find a solution."

There was no doubt what his uncle was implying. He expected Darcy to get rid of his guests.

Darcy's sense of outrage was ready to spill over, but he kept a lid on it – barely.

"Lord Matlock, the party assembled here was at my invitation. I requested them expressly to ride up from Town to stay here." Strictly speaking, that was not true of Elizabeth, but he wasn't about to split hairs over it. "What do you expect me to do about it, now that they are here?"

"I have heard the inn at Lambton is quite good," said Lady Matlock, helpfully.

"They serve a good mutton ragout there," said Lord Matlock. "I have had it on occasion, when your father was alive."

An icy anger swept through Darcy. He knew he needed to control his temper, but his uncle was going too far this time.

"Do you really expect me to ask my invited guests to leave and stay at an *inn*?"

"Only until we have left," said Lady Matlock, sweetly. "Though it may not be a bad idea to get rid of them altogether." She leaned forward in a half-whisper. "They really are rather common. All of them, with one exception. It does appear that Miss Bennet at least is a gentleman's daughter. Unfortunately, she is the only one with such a claim. As for the Gardiners – do you know the uncle not only actually works in trade, but apparently, he even lives within view of his own warehouse."

She pursed her lips in disgust and gave a quick nod, as if that clinched the matter. The Fitzwilliams had obviously wasted no time delving into the background of every one of the attendees. How they had done so when their food had been take up to their room he could only imagine. No doubt coins had changed hands.

"You do realize you have put us in an awkward situation," said Lord Matlock. "You can hardly expect us to acknowledge our social inferiors.

However, we cannot possibly confine ourselves to our rooms throughout our stay, particularly at dinner time."

"May I remind you that I did not put you in this situation? It is a situation you created yourself. While I acknowledge your right to arrive unannounced any time you wish – you will always be welcome at Pemberley – you cannot reasonably expect that I will cast my invited guests into the street at your convenience, Uncle. I have no objection to you staying as long as you wish. It is your prerogative; but you must accept that the situation may not always be entirely to your liking."

"Well, I never!" said Lady Matlock, rising to her feet. "I am appalled, nephew, and most seriously displeased. However, for Georgiana's sake I will not pick a quarrel with you. I would not wish my dear niece to be the loser in all this. She is in dire need of a motherly presence."

Darcy was too civil to point out that there was nothing remotely motherly about Lady Matlock, but he marveled at people's ability to delude themselves.

"I do hope you are planning to join us for dinner tonight," Darcy remarked. "I do not wish my guests to think you are snubbing them."

Lady Matlock swept out of the library. Lord Matlock lingered for a few minutes longer.

"You must not upset Lady Matlock, Darcy. She suffers from ill health, you know."

Darcy almost wished it were true, for then she would be far less likely to be so forceful in her opinions and to expend so much energy interfering in other people's business.

Georgiana withdrew into the billiards room as soon as the library door opened and the voices of their uncle and aunt drifted down the corridor. She had learned long ago that the best strategy to combat the Fitzwilliam's inevitable tendency to rule her life was to remain as invisible as possible. She waited impatiently for them to go upstairs and out of sight then hurried to the library to catch William.

He emerged from the room just as she reached the door and they almost collided in the corridor.

He had a particularly stormy look on his face, and for a moment she questioned the wisdom of talking to him when he was in such a mood. The problem could not wait, however – he needed to address it as soon as possible, before any damage was done.

"William, wait!" she said, as he gave her a tight nod and walked straight past her. "I must speak to you."

"Not now, Georgiana. This is not a good moment. I am looking for Bingley. Have you seen him?"

"I believe he has gone fishing with Mr. Hurst," said Georgiana, "But you cannot join them yet. What I have to say is *important*," said Georgiana. She was not going to give him a chance to say no.

For a moment he looked as if he was going to refuse her anyway, then he sighed and gave her a small smile.

"Come, then, let us go somewhere private where no one can overhear us."

She threw him a questioning look.

"It seems the Fitzwilliams have a spy – or several spies – in the household who have no scruples revealing everything that happens under this roof."

Georgiana stopped walking and examined him closely. "Oh – they have not revealed anything about *that* matter, have they?"

"No, of course not," replied her brother reassuringly. "You must not forget that no one at Pemberley knows anything about it, not even Mrs. Reynolds. But someone has been passing on gossip about our guests."

Darcy was walking very quickly. She had to practically run to keep up with him. The Fitzwilliams had clearly upset him. She had heard them arguing with him yesterday and now again this morning, though she had not heard what the argument was about.

"Where are we going, William?"

"To the orangery. No one ever goes there except the two of us and some of the gardeners."

It was the wrong place to go on a warm day, especially when they had guests. Her hair was already wilting. The level of humidity was uncomfortably high. Yet, as soon as she stepped inside and the heavy aroma of plants and soil embraced her, her mind felt somehow clearer.

"Do you remember how you used to hide from Father here when you were in trouble?"

She nodded. "You used to come and look for me, and then you would intercede with papa on my behalf." She looked sad. "I wish father was still with us."

"I only wish you remembered mama. You were too young to know what she was like. She would have been happy with the way you have turned out."

Georgiana leaned over and planted a quick kiss on his cheek.

"She would have been especially proud of you," she said.

They settled on their usual bench, under the lemon tree.

"William, I have something particular to say to you—"

Darcy interrupted.

"First let me reveal what I have to say because it concerns you directly. I did not originally intend to say anything, but after reflection I feel you ought to have an opportunity to express your opinion."

"Now you are making me curious."

"I do not think you will like what I have to say. Our aunt and uncle have taken it upon themselves to find you a husband and I am sorry to say they have succeeded. They are here to arrange your betrothal. To the Duke of Bolton."

A cry escaped her before she could stop herself. "The Duke of Bolton? The one who is always in the gossip columns about one mistress or the other?"

"I do not read the gossip columns," said Darcy, "And neither should you. But it would not surprise me to discover he had a mistress or two. Which wouldn't signify as it is an arranged marriage and one would hardly expect a duke – especially a duke who is often in the company of the Prince Regent – to be a model of faithful domesticity."

Georgiana felt as if a cold wind had swept into her heart.

She looked down at the tips of her slippers that were peeping from under her dress. "So is that to be my future?" her voice felt as if it was coming from far away.

Darcy leaned over and tipped up her chin.

"Silly sister," he said affectionately, using a term he had not used for a long time with her. "Do you honestly believe I would ever consent to such a thing?"

She threw her arms around his neck and buried her face in his shoulder. "Oh, William. I was so afraid you would." She hugged him tightly, not wanted to let go. His dark blue superfine coat seemed so familiar, so safe. But she was not a child anymore, and she could not hug him forever.

"So that was why you were quarrelling yesterday! Did you really stand up to the two of them?"

"I did, though I suspect it is far from over yet. They may try to find a way to browbeat you into submission. Do not let them do it. Stand your ground. Simply throw all the responsibility on me. Tell them it is not up to you, it is up to me, since I am your guardian. This is a good time to pretend to have no opinions or mind of your own."

"Oh. I did not know I *had* a mind of my own," said Georgiana.

Darcy gave her a disbelieving look then realized she was joking. "Since when have you turned into a jester?

"Since I realized the sky will not fall down on me if I make a joke," said Georgiana. "And since I discovered my brother is rather fond of laughter." She threw him a significant glance.

"Now you know my secret, I suppose you will confront me with it at every turn."

"No, only when you do not laugh at my jokes."

They had unintentionally come back to the very topic she wished to discuss. Darcy's choice of a wife.

"William, I have a warning of my own to impart. You *must* speak to Caroline and discourage her from thinking you intend to offer for her. Miss Bennet is convinced you intend to announce your engagement to Caroline any moment.

Darcy turned pale.

"Miss Bennet?" he said. "Is that—"

His mouth opened and closed and for a moment Georgiana thought he was about to collapse. She felt sorry now that she had brought the subject up. If she had known he would get so worked up about it—.

Understanding dawned. So that was why he had been behaving so strangely lately, and no wonder!

She grasped her hands together in surprise.

"William! You are in love with Miss Bennet!"

Darcy's pallor transformed in an instant into a dark shade of red.

"Hush, Georgiana. If my uncle hears of this—"

So Miss Bennet was his choice of a bride. How very strange. No wonder he had been so hesitant. She would certainly not win the approval of the Fitzwilliams, nor of Aunt Catherine. Miss Elizabeth Bennet was genteel and well bred, but she had heard Mr. Gardiner speak quite openly of business affairs that needed taking care of, so she knew the family had close connections to commerce. She was definitely not the kind of bride Darcy had been searching for at all.

All that fuss about the folded bit of paper with the list, and this is who he had chosen.

She clapped her hands and began to laugh.

"Oh, this is so incredible. I would never have thought it in a million years! Miss Elizabeth Bennet!"

"I fail to see what is so amusing." Darcy was so stiff he could have been a wall, except his ears were bright pink along with his face and his neck.

"You are, my dear brother," said Georgiana. "And all this time I thought you did not have a romantic bone in your body!"

~~X~~

Darcy did not have the opportunity to speak to Caroline until later in the day. When he reached the area of the garden where Georgiana had last seen Caroline and Elizabeth, they were nowhere to be found. He searched for them for some time, fearing that Caroline had taken the opportunity of their being alone to make her revelation, but they seemed to have disappeared into thin air.

It was not until after luncheon that he was able to approach her.

"Miss Bingley. Might I have a word with you? I have something of particular importance I must convey to you."

Caroline gave a saucy smile.

"You need not be quite so formal, you know, Mr. Darcy. Did you wish to see me in private?"

"No. I would prefer to speak to you in the presence of my sister. I have asked her to wait for us in the small parlor."

Caroline's confusion was evident.

"But—" she began. Then, as if acknowledging that it would not be wise to say too much: "Oh, very well. I am all agog to discover what it is you have to say."

She would not have been so eager if she knew what he intended to tell her.

Darcy felt like a cad. He was about to shatter her illusions, and he knew he played a role in – unintentionally – allowing them to develop. His visit to London, certainly, had only served to reinforce her belief that he was on the verge of a proposal.

He had been such a fool, a blind, appallingly selfish fool, and Caroline had been one of the victims. He should have put an end to her hopes a long time ago, but the truth was, he wanted to have her there as a standby, just in case. He had actually considered the possibility of marrying her not too long ago.

He needed to set her free to pursue someone else – someone who would care for her and appreciate the many good qualities she had.

When they entered the parlor Georgiana was sitting in a corner of the room engaged in some sewing. She looked up briefly when they entered, blushed, and resumed her work. No other sound permeated the room other than the laughter of several of the guests who were engaged in archery practice.

Darcy was immediately distracted by the sound of Elizabeth laughing. He made his way to the window discreetly, trying not to reveal his interest.

"You are in love with Eliza Bennet, are you not?" said Caroline, wryly.

Darcy turned, trying to determine whether to answer the question or not. Then he thought that the least he could do was be honest with her.

He nodded. "Yes."

There was nothing further to say about it.

"Then I wish you good fortune and happiness, although I can only foresee problems ahead for you. Your relatives will make your life difficult, you know. I have heard how Lady Matlock speaks to her. They will likely refuse to receive you in their home. You might wish to consider that you will be sacrificing a great deal and receiving little in return. At least I would have provided you with a considerable fortune."

"I will be receiving Elizabeth Bennet. That is all I want."

Caroline gave a pale smile. "Spoken like a man truly in love."

She rose to her feet. "Well then, if you will excuse me, I must take my leave. I hope you will not be offended if I leave for Town in the morning. I fear I will not be good company for the next few days."

Darcy could not help but admire the dignified manner in which she had handled his revelation. He went to her and took her hands in his.

"I am sorry, Caroline. I wish it could have been otherwise."

She nodded her head and, withdrawing her hands quickly, turned away, but not before Darcy had seen the glitter of tears in her eyes. Overcome by emotion, she hurried from the room.

Darcy watched her go. He understood her pain only too well, and he was sorry to have been the cause of it.

"You did the right thing, Brother," said Georgiana.

He started. He had forgotten his sister's presence completely.

He ran his hand through his hair. "Why does everything have to be so complicated? Why couldn't I have fallen in love with Caroline instead of Elizabeth?"

The answer hung in the air only long enough for Darcy to hear Elizabeth's laughter drifting in through the open window. It was like a rope pulling him in. He could no more resist it than he could prevent himself breathing.

"Well, little sister, now that I have done what you asked of me, would you be so kind as to accompany me to the garden?"

"Since you asked in such a gentlemanly fashion, William," said Georgiana. "How could I possibly refuse?"

But as she placed her hand through his arm, she turned serious.

"I hope we will continue to see Caroline in the future. I will miss her if we lose her friendship.

"I hope so, too," said Darcy, but his thoughts were already somewhere else.

Chapter Eighteen

It was not meant to be, Darcy decided. He was never to be allowed an opportunity to spend time alone with Elizabeth Bennet. For no sooner had Darcy and Georgiana reached the area where the archery had been set up than the footman came down the gravel path to announce that they had visitors.

Darcy stifled a growl as he heard the names. Surely Fate must be in collusion against him? Now he would also have to guard against Miss Marshall saying anything in front of Elizabeth.

He steeled himself to deal with the situation as best he could.

Beside him Georgiana tensed up as well.

Fortunately, there was enough time for him to assume a friendly expression while the three ladies paraded down the gravel path to where he stood.

"Mrs. Renwick. Mrs. Marshall. Miss Marshall. This is an unexpected pleasure, so soon after seeing you in London. What brings you to Derbyshire?"

The answer was obvious to anyone with half a mind. Georgiana had tried to warn him, but he had refused to acknowledge it. Miss Marshall was here expressly to capture him.

Well, he had put himself in this mess. He would have to extricate himself.

"Town has become so stiflingly hot. I could not bear it a moment longer," remarked Mrs. Marshall. "Then Mrs. Renwick wrote a letter insisting that my chances of recovery were far better in the countryside – I was ill for a while, you know – I was more than ready to escape from the unpleasant odors and the noise. The country is so much more restful, is it not? Tell Mr. Darcy what you said to me, Elinor."

For a moment, Miss Marshall looked perplexed. Then she seemed to understand what her mother wanted.

"I told mama that if she travelled the whole wide world, she would not find air as clear and fresh as the air at Pemberley."

Darcy bowed in acknowledgement.

"I hope we have not come visiting at an inconvenient time," said Mrs. Marshall. "I see you have a house party."

She threw him an accusing glance as if to berate him for holding a house party without her knowledge.

"Only a few friends from Town, Mrs. Marshall. Very informal."

At that moment his uncle scored a bull's eye, and there was a scattering of applause.

"Bravo!" cried Bingley. "Your lordship is a capital shot." Apparently Bingley had abandoned Hurst to his fishing and come to join the crowd.

"Well done, sir," called out Darcy, surprised to see Lord Matlock had condescended to join in the activity. He turned back to Mrs. Renwick. "You are acquainted with Lord and Lady Matlock?" he asked.

"Yes, of course I am."

"Then, if you will allow me, I would like to introduce Mrs. and Miss Marshall to Lady Matlock."

"That would be delightful," said Mrs. Marshall.

Since the Marshalls moved in similar circles to those of his uncle, there was a chance they would keep each other occupied.

He looked towards Elizabeth. He might yet find a way to steal some time with her without anyone noticing – if he could convince her to join him.

Mrs. Gardiner was now preparing to take up the bow and arrow and, from the good natured laughter of those watching, Darcy guessed she was a novice at archery.

He paused to watch, and to cast a look around for Elizabeth.

"Aren't you going to join us, Mr. Darcy?" said Elizabeth, approaching him from behind. "Or are you afraid you will find the competition too fierce?"

Mrs. Gardiner's arrow flew wide of the mark and into a tree. Elizabeth laughed delightedly at his side.

He drank in the sight of her. Her laughing eyes enchanted him, bewitched him. They made his pulse race and took away his breath. They left him too tongue-tied to say anything. He was forced to gesture helplessly with his hand towards the spot in the shade where Lady Matlock sat at the table looking thoroughly bored.

The laughter in her eyes died. "Yes, I see. You are otherwise occupied."

No, that is not it at all, he wanted to object. As usual, she had wilfully misunderstood him.

"I will return," said Darcy, finding the words at last. "And when I do, you had better beware."

Her lips twitched.

"Are you issuing a challenge, Mr. Darcy?"

"You may interpret it any way you wish," he said, laughter welling up inside him. He felt a pair of eyes bore into him. He turned to find Mrs. Marshall was watching him strangely.

"Shall we continue?" he said, politely waving them in the direction of Lady Matlock. He could hardly wait to rid himself of them and return to the woman he loved.

"Miss Marshall is very interested in archery, are you not, Elinor?" prompted Mrs. Marshall.

Miss Marshall looked flustered, but she did not miss her cue. "Mama, you know very well I don't know one end of the bow from the other." Her mother gave her a pointed look. "But I have always *wanted* to learn. More than anything." She drew closer to Darcy and took his free arm. "It is just that I never found the right gentleman to teach me. However, I am certain that if *you* were to teach me, you would find me a quick learner."

"I would be happy to teach you," said Georgiana, suddenly, from his other side. "I am considered quite a competent archer."

Darcy turned to look at his sister in surprise. She was looking obstinate. He did not know what to make of it. Was his little sister *protecting* him from Miss Marshall?

"Charming of you to offer, Miss Darcy," came the reply, "but surely you are too busy ordering refreshments and seeing to your other visitors' comfort? It is quite a responsibility hosting a House Party, is it not?"

177

Two familiar red blotches appeared on Georgiana's cheeks. Darcy recognized the signs; he was beginning to think of those blotches as war paint. "Of course, but that does not occupy all my time. Besides, since you are a visitor yourself, surely it is part of my duty to accommodate your every wish. I shall teach you to shoot, since you have expressed your interest. It is the least I can do."

Miss Marshall had forgotten to be haughty and distant and was glaring daggers at his sister. Georgiana – little, shy Georgiana – stood her ground.

It was up to him to declare a ceasefire.

"I do believe Lady Matlock is waving at us to join her," he said, practically dragging the two ladies forward by the arms. "I am far too hot and thirsty for archery at the moment. Let us find a seat in the shade. Why not have some refreshments and then we can decide what to do? Perhaps some of the group might have other suggestions for amusement – going for a walk, for example?"

"How very kind of you to accommodate me, Mr. Darcy," said Miss Marshall.

Darcy's prospects of stealing a moment alone with Elizabeth were rapidly evaporating. He could not hide his head in the sand like an ostrich and pretend Miss Marshall would somehow disappear. Just a few days ago he had almost made up his mind to marry her. She was persistent. She would not let go of him easily.

Besides, he could not completely discount Miss Marshall yet. What if Elizabeth categorically refused to marry him? What if her opinion of him was unchanged?

Waiting for the right moment to talk to Elizabeth was not going to happen, not unless he took hold of things, firmly and with two hands, but how could he, when he did not know how she would react? He desperately needed to discover how she felt about him, but how was he to do that? He could not very well walk up to her and ask he if she cared for him, but that was precisely what he wanted to know.

There was only one way to find out and that was to propose to Elizabeth Bennet – again.

~~X~~

As the archery contest ended, the small group of contestants disbanded into different directions. From the Venetian tent set up for refreshments, Georgiana spotted Miss Marshall dragging William away to show her how to use a bow. William was looking harassed, but he could not deny her without being discourteous.

A moment later, her aunt waved to Miss Bennet to join the ladies and Georgiana felt a moment of sympathy for her.

Georgiana meanwhile was using the pretext of needing to oversee the servants as they laid out the refreshments to avoid the Marshalls, her aunt and her uncle.

"Do you know why Caroline was looking so grim a little while ago?" said Bingley. "I wonder if I ought to go in to see if there is something the matter."

Georgiana wondered if she should say anything, but in the end she decided it was not up to her to reveal what was, after all, a private matter.

"I believe she had some bad news," remarked Georgiana.

"Then I shall go and cheer her up," said Bingley, readily.

She turned away and busied herself shuffling cups and saucers, sandwich trays, and anything she could lay her hands on, though in reality everything was laid out perfectly for the guests.

Just then, Miss Bennet came towards her, looking distinctly vexed.

"Oh, you are just in time for the muscadine ice," said Georgian, handing her a bowl of ice. "The confectioner is most anxious we should eat it quickly. What do you think of it? Is it not perfect for this weather?"

"It is perfectly delicious, Miss Darcy. Thank you. It was just what I needed to cool me down. I fear I was becoming overheated."

"I do not suppose you are referring to the archery, Miss Bennet," said Georgiana with a little laugh, understanding her meaning at once.

"Indeed I am not! I was enjoying the archery," said Elizabeth Bennet, in a low voice, "until it finished and Lady Matlock ordered me most imperiously to join her and the Marshalls. Far be it for me to

179

engage in gossip, Miss Darcy, but in this case it is quite beyond my power to resist." She looked around her to make sure no one could overhear. "I am certain the three ladies were competing for a prize to see who could be the most condescending. Then your uncle joined us, and I believe the prize would have to go to him. I hope you do not mind my being so open with you. I have younger sisters like you, and I am accustomed to confiding in them. I do not wish to cause offence."

Georgiana smiled. "You cannot possibly cause offence, Miss Bennet. My uncle and aunt have long since been the bane of my existence. They have no knowledge of me at all; the only thing they care to know is whether I am pretty and well-mannered enough to catch a title, which they can then hang like a trophy to their family tree." What Darcy had told her regarding their plans for her marriage was only just sinking in. "Yet they insist on interfering at every turn. If my brother had listened to them, I would have been sent to live with a terrifying old lady who would have made my life miserable. Fortunately, both Darcy and my guardian, Colonel Fitzwilliam, who is their son, refused to give in to them. It resulted in a fearful row, but at the end I was sent to a girl's academy, where at least I spent some time with other girls my age. There are other occasions, too, when their interference would have changed my life for the worse. So you see, you cannot offend me no matter what you say about them."

"Goodness," said Miss Bennet. "I feel sorry for you, having to deal with such insufferable relations, with no mother or father to put a stop to it. It is fortunate in that case that your brother took his responsibilities seriously. Many young men would have not wished to concern themselves with a younger sister."

Georgiana's face darkened. "I think there was a time— Darcy was twenty when my father died. I understand now, as I did not then—well, he resented the responsibility he was saddled with—a huge estate to be managed and a young brat like me who did nothing but cry because she had lost her father. I think he was angry at the world. But later, as he grew accustomed to his responsibilities—I cannot fault him for a moment, except perhaps I would have wished to see more of him. But it is the same, is it not, when the boys go away to school and see little of their families for months at a time, is it not?

"It is hard to know what is best. It is what everyone does, but it cannot have been easy. You must have been lonely."

"I will admit to being lonely sometimes."

She felt shy, suddenly. She looked around the tent, becoming aware of where she was. She was not accustomed to confiding in anyone, just one or two girls who had been at school with her, but Miss Bennet made it surprisingly easy to do so.

Miss Bennet reached out, and to her surprise, put her arm around her shoulders.

"Well, I hope you will consider me a friend. I am not so very much older than you, you know. When I return home you must write to me and tell me how you are faring. And if you wish, you may come and stay with us. Longbourn is not a quarter as grand as Pemberley, and my sisters are noisy and ill-mannered, but it is very lively there, and you will enjoy it. What do you think?"

"I should like it very much."

Miss Bennet spoke as if she did not yet know of her brother's feelings. Was she not aware that in the future the two families could well be exchanging visits?

She felt herself smiling at the thought. Miss Bennet would be the perfect wife for William.

At that moment Lady Matlock came up to them. Clearly Miss Bennet had not yet escaped her clutches.

"I have been looking for you, Miss Bennet. Darcy wishes to go for a walk and I will not walk with any of the others. You must be my companion, Miss Bennet. In fact, I have been considering taking on a companion one of these days, and I have decided you will suit well enough. As I hear your family's circumstances are strained, this may be a good opportunity for you—"

"Lady Matlock, I am sorry if you have the wrong impression, but as I have told you, I am a gentleman's daughter and I have no need to take on a position of any kind. I consider your proposal an offence. Now if you will allow me, I wish to join the others in their walk."

With this, Miss Bennet walked away, leaving Lady Matlock staring after her in astonishment.

"I do not know what came over the chit. I thought she would be happy for assistance with her family finances."

Now that she knew that Darcy was considering Miss Bennet as a wife, Georgiana was shocked at her aunt's lack of sensitivity. How could she assume Miss Bennet would be happy to serve her? She had never felt so embarrassed in her life. What was her aunt thinking? Her heart swelled with indignation on behalf of her new friend.

"I think you have it all wrong, Aunt," she said, quacking a little in her half-boots but determined not to let her aunt intimidate her. "Miss Bennet is not in any need of assistance. She was touring Derbyshire with her aunt and uncle, who are very well to do. She has only just invited me to visit her estate. I consider it an honor to receive such an invitation, and I have accepted. Now if you will excuse me, I must join the others."

Shaking at her own audacity, Georgiana headed straight for the small knot of people that had gathered at the bridge, willing herself not to look back even though she could feel Lady Matlock's gaze like a spear driving into her.

Chapter Nineteen

It was an exemplary summer day, with just a hint of coolness in the air after a night of rain. Unfortunately, Darcy could not truly enjoy it. His palms were sweating as they gripped the bridle, and his heart was beating so erratically he wondered how Bingley could continue to converse in such an inane manner. Was Bingley really so blind as to notice he was not listening to anything his friend was saying?

Darcy could not remain silent a moment longer.

"Bingley, I hate to say it, but I have no interest at all today in the size of the fish you caught yesterday."

Bingley stopped in mid-sentence and stared at Darcy in astonishment.

"Come, Darcy. Was it really necessary to interrupt me in this rude manner?"

"Yes. I have far more important matters on my mind at the moment." He stopped and stared intently across the valley at Pemberley.

"I see. Perhaps you can enlighten me as to what you consider more important than fishing," said Bingley, with a laugh.

"I intend to offer for Miss Elizabeth Bennet today."

"Do you really?" said Bingley, delightedly. "Well then, admit it. You, too, wish to talk of fishing, but of a different kind."

"Knock it off, Bingley," said Darcy. "This is no time for joking. I am eaten up with anxiety. I have not much opportunity to speak to her, to determine her feelings towards me, but I sense that some of her resistance has thawed. Do you think it likely she might be more receptive than the first time?"

"It depends entirely on how you phrase it. If you are going to lecture her about being from an unworthy family—"

Darcy growled. "I knew I should not have confided in you."

Bingley laughed. "It is too late now, Darcy. I am privy to all your secrets."

"Then the least you could do is help me rehearse the words," said Darcy. "I bungled the job the first time. I do not wish to do so again."

"I would be happy to do so. If you agree to do the same for me when I offer for Miss Bennet."

"With pleasure, Bingley. I cannot imagine anyone else I would prefer to have as a brother."

Bingley beamed. "Well then, let us hear what you have to say."

Darcy felt profoundly self-conscious as he began. "Dearest Elizabeth—"

"No, no!" said Bingley. "I know you are good at letter-writing, but this is not a letter."

The interruption disrupted Darcy's flow and he promptly forgot everything he had meant to say.

"Could you kindly listen to the whole thing first before intervening?"

They now had a view of the road and he noticed a carriage just about to disappear into Pemberley Woods.

Darcy frowned. "Someone is leaving. I wonder who? Can you see the coat of arms on the carriage?"

"Not without a spy-glass. My sisters were speaking of leaving this morning, but I doubt either of them is up yet. Besides, the carriage is the wrong color. In any case, I do not know how you can be sure it is someone leaving. Mrs. Gardiner was saying something about going to Meryton by carriage today."

"I offered her the use of my carriage. Besides, if you were going into Meryton, would you load up with luggage?"

"I would not, but I cannot speak for everyone. I have heard stranger things."

A moment's thought revealed that the only people likely to depart without saying goodbye were the Fitzwilliams. No doubt they had decided they no longer wished to consort with Persons of Inferior Background and decided to return home.

"I think it is most likely certain personages who consider everyone beneath them. Good riddance."

"I suppose you mean your aunt and uncle?" said Bingley. "Did they inform you they were planning to depart?"

184

"No, they did not, but it does not surprise me at all. They consider themselves a law unto themselves."

"They were not happy to have us here, were they?"

Darcy considered hiding the truth, then decided he did not want to conceal things from Bingley any more.

"They were not. But let us not speak of the Fitzwilliams. There are other matters I wish to deal with. Come, let us go in the shade of the tree and I can rehearse my proposal."

~~x~~

It took Bingley so long to approve Darcy's proposal that Darcy was ready to give up. The small corrections he kept making drove Darcy to the edge of insanity. Only the fact that – as Bingley pointed out – he would never again have the opportunity to repeat his offer if she refused him this time kept him going.

"Are you sure you don't wish to take a glass of Madeira before you start, for Dutch courage?"

"No, I am fired up enough as it is," said Darcy.

Never had he felt such an agitation of spirits as today. His stomach was tied up in so many knots he was sure it would never unravel again. His worry was a physical ache.

If she turned him down.

He could not think of that. Surely now that she had been here, seen how he lived – but of course that would not make an iota of difference if she still disliked him. And therein lay the rub.

He did not know how she felt. He had sensed a softening of attitude towards him in the way she looked at him, but considering how mistaken he had been the first time, he could not trust himself to get it right.

"Brother," said Georgiana with concern. "Why are you clutching your stomach like that? Are you unwell?"

"He's well enough," said Bingley. "He just has a private matter to attend to."

Georgiana blushed and looked from one to another. "Did I say the wrong thing? Was I hideously embarrassing?"

"Ignore Bingley. He is deriving a great deal of amusement from my discomfort."

As if to prove it, Bingley burst into laughter. "Darcy, you can be hare-brained sometimes. You have given your sister the impression that your discomfort is based on the demands of nature."

"Demands of—?" As he realized what Bingley was referring to, his face grew warm.

"I do not need the privy," he said. "That is not the private matter I was referring to." He took a deep breath. "I am very hopeful that you will approve of what I am about to do. I am about to propose to Miss Elizabeth Bennet."

Georgiana put a hand to her mouth in dismay.

Darcy's belief in his capacity to understand others received a shock. If he did not understand Georgiana, what hope was there of understanding anyone? "I had the impression you liked her."

"Miss Bennet?" Georgiana was looking distressed. "Of course I like her, but that is neither here nor there. I am afraid it is too late."

"What do you mean? Is she engaged to be married?"

If that was the case, that he had missed proposing to her by a few minutes because he was rehearsing his piece—

"No, nothing like that, but I'm sorry to tell you, she left one hour ago."

"What did they say? Surely they did not leave without a word?"

"Mrs. Gardiner said Mr. Gardiner had received news requiring him to return home unexpectedly – something concerning a business matter."

"Of course he would say that," said Darcy, agitatedly. "It is my uncle and aunt, is it not? They were the ones who drove them away."

"We cannot be certain of that," said Georgiana, hesitantly. "I do know Miss Bennet was vexed with them yesterday, and very rightly so, as Lady Matlock was particularly insulting, but would that be enough to make them all leave? Surely they would not be so ill-mannered to depart like this on a small slight."

186

"Depend upon it," said Darcy. "The Fitzwilliams have insulted the Gardiners by speaking disparagingly of trade."

"You do not know that," said Georgiana, soothingly, feeling instinctively that to tell him of Lady Matlock's offer of employment would add fuel to the fire. "In any case, Mrs. Gardiner has left a note for you."

She produced a folded paper from her reticule.

"Why did you not say so earlier?"

"I have not yet had the chance."

Darcy grasped the letter from her and broke the seal impatiently.

Dear Mr. Darcy,

I am sorry to leave you so suddenly. I fear it is but a poor repayment of your hospitality. However, unfortunately Mr. Gardiner has heard news of a most urgent nature and he will not hear of postponing his trip despite the lingering effects of the accident.

I take my most humble leave with many thanks to you and Miss Darcy for all your efforts on our behalf.

Most sincerely,

M. Gardiner

Darcy crumpled up the note and tossed it to the floor.

"What does it say?" asked Bingley.

"That's just it. It says nothing at all. No explanation, nothing more than a vague apology. What could be so urgent that they could not have waited an hour or two to take their leave? I am not even sure the repairs to their carriage have been completed."

"There must be a reasonable explanation," said Bingley.

"You have heard what Georgiana has to say," said Darcy, gesturing towards her. "It is my uncle and aunt. They have gone too far this time. I shall have to ask them to leave."

"Pray do not, William," said Georgiana. "If it is unrelated then you will upset our uncle for nothing." He heard her words through a haze of anger, not really comprehending them.

187

"I think you should take a few minutes to collect yourself before you do anything you might regret," said Bingley. "You are not one to take action on an impulse."

Impulse. The word breached the haze. He had promised himself to forsake any impulsive actions. He would do well to heed Bingley's – and Georgiana's – advice.

"Very well," he said, as the haze of anger cleared.

The anger faded, but not the sense of bitter disappointment. He had been planning to propose to Miss Bennet and now the opportunity had been snatched away from him.

He could bring her back. If he followed them and apologized abjectly for his relatives' behavior. Perhaps that would be the best plan.

"I will go after them," said Darcy. "I imagine I know where they will stop for the night. I will go and reason with them to return."

"No, Darcy," said Bingley, but he was already ascending the stairs to inform his valet to pack an overnight bag.

In his chamber, he rang the bell-pull vigorously and paced the room as he waited. Every second seemed an interminable delay, but he would look foolish if he was not prepared to stay the night. It was unlikely he would catch up with them before they had gone too far to return the same day.

Where the devil was Briggs when he needed him? At this rate he would probably have to pack his clothes himself.

Briggs appeared in the doorway, not a moment too soon.

"What took you so long?" said Darcy, knowing he was being unreasonable but unable to be anything else.

He had prepared his proposal, for heaven's sake.

The little man shook his head and tut-tutted. "Is this about Miss Bennet's departure?" he said, with his usual impertinence. Really, Darcy did not know why he kept the man on. He was a menace.

"It is none of your concern," said Darcy.

"Of course not, sir," said Briggs, blandly. "Though I do wonder what was in that express of hers."

Darcy stopped in his tracks and stared at him.

"What express?"

"The one that was delivered to her this morning, sir. Jenny, Miss Georgiana's maid, said that when Miss Bennet read it, she burst into tears and ran to find her aunt. Bad news from home, I would imagine."

Darcy sat down on the bed with a thump. So that was what it was all about. He felt giddy with relief. So there was a good reason for the sudden departure. It was not something that he or his family had done.

Thank heavens he had not thrown out the Fitzwilliams.

Then, as the import of Brigg's news finally reached him, he thought of Elizabeth. What if her father or mother had suddenly taken ill? Or worse. It would have had to be grim for them to depart so instantly when poor Mr. Gardiner had barely recovered from his injury.

He would write the Gardiners a letter of enquiry immediately – possibly even go to Netherfield if he felt Elizabeth was in need of his support.

"I asked you, sir, why did you ring for me?"

From the doubtful way Briggs was looking at him, he assumed that the little valet had already asked him that question earlier.

"I have changed my mind. However, I do wish to know something. How the devil do you manage to know everything that is happening in this household before anyone else does?"

The valet shrugged. "You could say it's a talent of mine, sir."

Darcy gave him a hard look. "You have not been making use of this talent of yours to make a few extra coins on the side, have you? From Lady Matlock, for example."

"Heaven forbid, Mr. Darcy. I know she's your relation and all that, but I would rather not go anywhere near her."

Darcy examined his valet. He did not quite know whether to believe him, but Briggs' uncanny ability to ferret out information had come in handy on several occasions.

"Very well, then. I have not yet made up my mind what I wish to do yet. I may call you to pack later."

"As you wish, sir." Briggs bowed and left.

Darcy made his way slowly downstairs.

189

He was vastly relieved that it was no fault of his own that had caused Elizabeth to leave, but his sense of frustration had returned.

Even if he sent an express to the Gardiners, they would not receive it until they arrived in town tomorrow at the earliest, and who knows how quickly they would reply. He wished he could take off after them, but it would hardly be appropriate, particularly if a tragedy had occurred in the family.

He could do nothing at this point. He would simply have to wait and hope the Gardiners would not choose to keep him in suspense for too long.

~~X~~

Three days later, he had not yet heard from the Gardiners. He did what he could to keep himself occupied, but he lived in a state of fevered anxiety. He had come so close to making Elizabeth his own; he felt as if consigned to purgatory, his fate hanging in the balance.

The Gardiners had not yet answered. Whatever the reason for their departure may be, they at least owed him the courtesy of replying. He could not help feeling there was more to it than that. Something had unquestionably happened. There was no doubt of that. But perhaps they had taken it as an opportunity to sever all ties with him after being subjected to Lady Matlock's insults. He could not help feeling he had not done enough to shield Elizabeth from them. He ought to have asked them to leave before they had done any damage.

Well, the Fitzwilliams had left, after a titanic quarrel during which Darcy had refused categorically to permit Georgiana's marriage to the elderly Duke of Bolton. Caroline and her sister had also left, with Caroline plainly holding her tattered pride together with an effort. Only Bingley and Mr. Hurst remained, and Darcy was enormously grateful for their company – at least he could play billiards with them, and fish in their company, and play cards. Not that it was quite enough to distract him, but far better than being left alone in a state of heightened expectation.

On the fourth day, a letter did finally arrive in the afternoon. The handwriting was familiar – the pointed, bold lettering belonging to Lady Catherine was unmistakable. Contrary to his custom of always dealing with all his correspondence immediately, he set it aside, resentful of all his relations, not at all desirous of reading it. It was undoubtedly a repetition of her earlier request to be put in charge of Georgiana's Season, and he did not have the patience to deal with his aunt at this particular moment. He tossed it to the bottom of his drawer and went to play billiards with Bingley.

The next day, however, another missive arrived, this time from Mr. Collins. The coincidence of two letters arriving from Hunsford in such close proximity in time was enough to prompt Darcy to open his aunt's letter.

Dear Nephew,

A report of a most alarming nature has reached me concerning the family of a young lady with whom you are acquainted. It appears that the youngest of the Bennet girls has eloped with Wickham and, what is worse, it seems they have not gone to Gretna Green.

I feel it expedient upon me to inform you of this matter at once, since, deceived by her character, I committed the error of inviting Miss Elizabeth Bennet to visit Rosings. You may as well know that her family is in Disgrace, and that she and her four sisters are utterly ruined in the eyes of the world. I am not entirely surprised at such an outcome. As you may recall, I expressed my opinions forcibly on the upbringing and neglect of the Bennet girls when Miss Bennet was at Rosings. The misfortune of five girls with no brother was bad enough; to have the younger girls out at that same time as their elders was the height of folly and indulgence.

I told Miss Bennet as much. Had Miss Elizabeth Bennet conveyed my advice to her mother as soon as she had returned home to Meryton, they would not now be facing such a situation.

I have, naturally, instructed Mr. Collins to send a missive of condolence to the Bennet family on this most tragic occasion, with instructions about how best they are to conduct themselves under the circumstances. A female's virtue is her most precious possession. Once

191

lost, it is lost forever. In circumstances such as these, it would be
infinitely preferable for the culprit to be dead than to for her to bring
such ruin and desolation to her sisters. I am certain by now she has
bitterly regretted her folly, but since nothing can redeem her ignominy
there is little to be done about it.

Under the circumstances all communication with this young woman
of inferior birth and circumstances, and with any members of her family,
must cease immediately. We cannot be tarnished with the same brush.
You must consider Anne's reputation; I am certain you wish her standing
to be spotless when you take her as your bride.

Your devoted aunt,
Catherine de Bourgh

Darcy's heart clenched as he finished reading. He threw the letter down on the desk, horrified, angered and ashamed all at once. The speed at which his aunt wished to disclaim any acquaintance with Miss Bennet astounded him. Her selfishness, her complete inability to comprehend the feelings of others, was brought home to him more than strikingly than ever before. How could she abandon the Bennets so completely when misfortune struck?

How Elizabeth must be feeling now! No wonder she had left so quickly, avoiding all explanations. It was hardly surprising that the Gardiners had not answered his express. For what could they say, after all? What explanation could they give?

Wondering now what Mr. Collins had to say, and conscious that Mrs. Collins was Elizabeth's particular friend, Darcy opened the next letter hoping to hear more of an explanation.

Dear Mr. Darcy,
I feel myself called upon by my duty to write at once to offer you my
most abject apologies. I am certain you by now have received news of the
scandalous event that has befallen the Bennet family, and which I
dutifully reported to your most estimable aunt, Lady Catherine. Since my
dear Charlotte revealed the news to me, I have been distraught at the
blame I fear you and your most gracious aunt may attach to me. I feel it

incumbent upon me to express my utmost remorse on having received this Person into my house and consequently having brought this Person into your presence. I wish there to be no doubt in your mind that I would not have offended my esteemed patroness Lady Catherine de Bourgh for anything, nor sullied your noble personage with such an association, had I known that such an appalling occurrence was impending. Rest assured that neither she nor any member of her family will be received forthwith at the Parsonage. As I am sure you are only too aware, this false step in one daughter will be injurious to the fortunes of all the others; for who, as her ladyship herself has condescended to say to me, will wish to connect themselves with such a family henceforth? None of the ladies of the house can now have any hopes of marriage. In my role as a clergyman and their cousin, I must expend every possible effort to distance myself from that family. As for the culprit who brought such ignominy on her family, she must be abandoned and left to reap the fruits of her own heinous offence.

I am, dear sir, and will remain always, your most humble servant,
William Collins

Darcy was so incensed by Mr. Collins' letter that he was tempted to travel down to Kent immediately to wring the wretched clergyman's neck. How dare he presume to pass judgment on Elizabeth like that? How dare he apologize for "sullying" him with Elizabeth's presence? As if her sister's elopement with Wickham made her any less desirable to him! And as for Mrs. Collins, whom he had thought a close friend of Elizabeth's, how could she have betrayed her friend by telling her husband the news, knowing he would immediately communicate it to Lady Catherine?

He felt the depth of that betrayal as if it was his own.

Nothing, nothing that anyone in her family did or said could ever make him love Elizabeth any less deeply than he loved her now, now that she had been wronged and cast away by the world for something that she did not even commit herself.

How could they even blame her sister, when it was Wickham who was the culprit? When Wickham, with no remorse or shame, for no *reason* at all, had destroyed the reputation of not only one very young girl but her four sisters as well? When Wickham had intended to do the very same thing with his sister, and it was only the good fortune of Darcy's arrival that had foiled the plot?

All his feelings of shame and remorse came to the fore.

This was his doing. His silence had brought this upon the Bennet family. He had been so intent on concealing Georgiana's near-disastrous episode with Wickham from the world that he had never thought of revealing Wickham's true nature. He should at least have attempted to warn the inhabitants of Meryton not to be deceived by Wickham's charm and good looks, but he had been too busy proving his own superiority to care what befell them. He was entirely to blame for the Bennet's disgrace, for all the scandal and misfortune that was befalling them.

Darcy jumped to his feet. What use was it, to be sitting here at his desk, blaming himself, when he should be at Elizabeth's side? She needed him. They all needed him to help them weather the storm.

He would go to Meryton at once and he would make amends by proving that he, at least, would be at their side, no matter what happened.

Chapter Twenty

"What is that disagreeable man doing here?" said Mrs. Bennet.

Darcy pressed his lips together grimly. Darcy wished hers was not the first voice he was hearing upon arriving at Longbourn, but, aside from covering his ears, he could think of no way to avoid it. The windows were open and, since he stood right underneath them, he could distinguish each word as clearly as if he was in the room.

"I vow, any friend of Mr. Bingley's will always be welcome here, to be sure; but I must say that I hate the very sight of him. And why did he not bring Mr. Bingley with him, I'd like to know? He's here to gloat over our misfortune, I am certain of it, and to give himself airs," said Mrs. Bennet. "He and that odious Mr. Collins must be laughing at us, discussing how fortunate it would be if Mr. Wickham were to kill Mr. Bennet in a fight. Mr. Bennet may say all he chooses, but I know he does not have the strength to fight against a seasoned soldier like Wickham. He will be hacked all to bits, and then what shall become of us? Oh, my poor nerves!"

So Mrs. Bennet disliked him, did she? It was certainly mutual. Yet to think that she believed him capable of making a mockery of their family's distress – how poor her opinion of him must be! Had he really provoked such ill feeling in Meryton by his behavior? Once more his sense of shame came to the fore.

He could hear indistinct voices murmuring something soothing. He imagined one of them would have to be Elizabeth's.

Mrs. Bennet's nerves were apparently sufficiently recovered for her to continue. "Tell that disagreeable man to go away as I shall *not* receive him."

So she was not willing to receive him, then? At least she did not dissemble and fawn on him as others in her situation would do. Still, it was the ultimate snub, and it rankled. He was not accustomed to being snubbed.

However, he had not come all the way to go down at the first hurdle. He was here for one reason and one reason only. He could not bear to have Elizabeth suffer for Wickham's perfidy. Wickham, who had almost destroyed Georgiana, had no scruples at all to run off with another gentleman's daughter, though what he thought he had to gain from it was entirely unclear. Darcy could understand Wickham's motives far better when it came to Georgiana. Revenge and greed were strong motives. In the case of Lydia Bennet, however, there could be no reason to ruin the reputation of a young girl hardly fifteen years old whose family had made him welcome. Vanity, perhaps, and a sense of power over a girl who was silly enough to fancy herself in love with him, were enough to overcome any scruples he might have had about completely ruining not only one of the Bennet girls but all of them, to have them ostracized from polite society and open to defamation and insult. It was hard to believe that the companion of his childhood had turned out to be so evil, so devoid of conscience that he could do such a thing.

He could attach very little blame to the young girl concerned. Lydia Bennet was giddy and completely lacking in sense. However, he could not blame her for being seduced by Wickham when his perfectly sombre, shy and retired sister had fallen under the villain's spell and was planning to do the same thing at exactly the same age. The blame must be placed squarely on the shoulders of their seducer.

Wickham was to blame. So was he – Fitzwilliam Darcy, if only indirectly. His pride had prevented him from admitting the truth of Wickham's villainy to the world. If he had warned the inhabitants of Meryton of Wickham's faults – then not only might Mr. Bennet have refused to consider sending Lydia to Brighton, but the shopkeepers who had provided goods and services in return for credit might not have been cheated of their money. Darcy alone had known of Wickham's character, yet had stood by and said nothing.

He was to blame, and he had to shoulder the responsibility.

He pulled his shoulders back, bracing himself, and reached for the knocker.

~~X~~

He was admitted into the room he remembered so very well by the housekeeper. The room had scarcely changed since he had last been here. The roses in a vase over the mantle. The small sewing table in the corner. The view of the large oak tree through the windows.

There was no one there.

"Someone will be with you presently, sir," said the woman, bobbing a curtsey.

He went over to the mantle and leaned his elbow on it in an effort to appear casual and to prevent himself from pacing.

By and by, the door opened and three of the Bennet sisters appeared. Miss Bennet, Miss Catherine and – Elizabeth.

She was as beautiful as ever. She had lost the bloom in her cheeks, but her eyes were large and intense in a face grown pale with anxiety. His heart lurched at the pain she must be enduring. Lydia's situation in society's eyes was worse than death, because at least death had a certain dignity to it. There was no hope for Lydia. She was lost to her family forever.

Darcy longed to run to Elizabeth, to take her in his arms and to kiss away all the pain. Jane's quiet presence fortunately forced him to control himself.

He bowed formally. "I was on my way to Rosings when I decided to call on you."

The sisters curtseyed and sat next to each other on a sofa.

"Thank you, Mr. Darcy." Elizabeth did not quite meet his gaze.

"When you left Pemberley so suddenly, I did not know why."

Elizabeth gave a helpless gesture. "I am sorry, circumstances beyond our control forced us to leave very suddenly. Did you receive my aunt's note?"

"Yes, thank you." He turned to address the eldest sister. "Miss Bennet, are you well?"

"Quite well," answered Miss Bennet.

He could do a good deed while he was here. Surely it wouldn't be considered improper.

"My friend Mr. Bingley wished me to convey his greetings." Darcy kept it deliberately vague, but he was looking at Miss Bennet.

She inclined her head and blushed prettily, a light rose color that diffused through her face. It was subtle enough that he might have missed it if he had not been paying attention. No wonder Elizabeth had said that Jane did not betray her feelings easily.

"And you, Miss Catherine, are you well."

"Oh, I am well enough, but with all the fuss—" she stopped abruptly as Miss Bennet must have pinched her arm.

He looked at Elizabeth gravely, pretending not to have noticed anything. "I wish to ascertain the truth of what my aunt, Lady Catherine has written to me," he said, trying not to allow Elizabeth's gaze to freeze his power of speech. He did not want to tell her that he had come all the way to Longbourn expressly to speak to her. "You and your uncle and aunt left Pemberley so abruptly I did not at first know the circumstances. I just wished to offer you my assistance in any way I can."

"That is very kind of you, Mr. Darcy, but I do not see what anyone can do under the circumstances." Elizabeth's embarrassment was plain to see. "My sister has been irreparably ruined, and we cannot force Wickham to marry her even if we knew where they were, which we do not. My father is honor-bound to challenge Wickham to a duel, but that will not accomplish anything, either, even if he were to win the fight, which is by no means certain. It will not restore Lydia's reputation, nor ours, for that matter."

"Do you have any idea of their location at least?"

"They have been traced as far as Clapham, but beyond that they could be anywhere." Elizabeth gave a hopeless shake of the head.

"My uncle believes they must be in London, but London is so large," said Jane, her countenance serene, but she was twisting a handkerchief tightly round her forefinger, so tightly that the tip had turned dark purple.

He looked at the young women before him, bravely facing the world, helpless in dealing with the blow that fate had visited upon them, unable to do anything to prevent the worst from happening.

He came to his feet, realizing that he might be the only hope for them. He had come to speak to Elizabeth, to assure her of his support, but he could do more. There was a chance at least that he may be able to trace Wickham's whereabouts. It was of the utmost importance for him to go to London at once.

"I must take my leave from you now, but I would like to assure you that you have my support," he said. He did not wish to give them false hope when nothing was certain.

"Thank you, Mr. Darcy," said Elizabeth.

He bowed and left, a sense of urgent determination seizing him.

~~x~~

As Darcy was settling onto his saddle, his hand brushed against the pocket of his waistcoat and he felt the edge of a piece of paper. The list. He had continued to carry it around with him wherever he went.

Perhaps he would still need it. Perhaps Elizabeth would still turn him down, no matter what.

He took it out of his pocket and read over the list of items he had written, so many of them scratched out, rewritten, or replaced.

For a moment, he hesitated. Then he tore it up to pieces and as he began to move, tossed it over his shoulder. The slight breeze picked the fragments and for a few seconds they drifted around, then fluttered to the ground like snow.

He would not need it again.

There was only one woman he wished for in his life, and he knew exactly what qualities she had.

He was not going to let her go, no matter what happened.

As he began to move, he made a pledge, to himself and to the woman he was determined to make his wife.

My dearest, bewitching Elizabeth, I give you my pledge of honor that I will do everything I can to restore your sister to you and to save her from Wickham, and that once I have achieved that I will be back, and then I will woo you as I have wanted to do for so long. I will take up residence in Meryton, and I will prove to every one of its inhabitants that they were mistaken in their opinion of me. I will devote every moment of my time in revealing my inner self to you until you become convinced that I am worthy of your love.

Until then, I will hold my love for you in my heart like a beacon to guide me and serve as a reminder for me to forgo my pride and be worthy of your good opinion.

This is my pledge to you.

To be continued...

To be informed when Volume 2 of The Darcy Novels comes out, please contact the author at one of the following:
Twitter: @Monica_Fairview
Facebook: http://www.facebook.com/monica.fairview

About The Author

Monica can be described as a gypsy-wanderer, opening her eyes to life in London and travelling ever since. She spent many years in the USA before coming back full circle to London, thus proving that the world is undeniably round.

Monica's first novel was *An Improper Suitor*, a humorous Regency. Since then, she has written two traditional Jane Austen sequels: *The Other Mr. Darcy* and *The Darcy Cousins* (both published by Sourcebooks) and contributed a sequel to *Emma* in Laurel Ann Nattress's anthology *Jane Austen Made Me Do It* (Ballantine). She has also published a futuristic *Pride and Prejudice* spin-off, *Steampunk Darcy*. *Mr. Darcy's Pledge* is the first volume of her series, *The Darcy Novels*, which are traditional *Pride and Prejudice* variations focusing on Darcy's transformation through his love for Elizabeth.

Monica Fairview is an ex-literature professor who abandoned teaching criticism about long gone authors who can't defend themselves in order to write novels of her own. Originally a lover of everything Regency, Monica has since discovered that the Victorian period can be jolly good fun, too, if seen with retro-vision and rose-colored goggles. She adores Jane Austen, Steampunk, cats, her husband and her impossible child.

If you'd like to find out more about Monica, you can find her at
Web page: www.monicafairview.com,
Blog: http://austenvariations.com,
Facebook: http://www.facebook.com/monica.fairview
Twitter @Monica_Fairview

Made in the USA
Middletown, DE
28 October 2023